PAPA'S SHADOW

G. R. O'Berry

SOUTHAMPTON COUNTY: 1932

The black Hudson rolled up the long lane. A narrow cloud of dust curled behind it and formed a white mist. The phantom auto chugged up the drive slowly: formidable and menacing. Papa was the first in the county to own an automobile and he always took his half of the road in the middle. Henry sat on the front porch, his insides percolating.

Henry was eighteen and angry—angry *and* scared. He was going to confront and if necessary, defy his Papa for the very first time. *I've been busting my ass on this farm since I was seven and I'm tired.* He had watched seven of his older siblings leave one by one: two sisters to marriage, one to college, and four older brothers, two to the military and two to college.

Henry had overheard a conversation between his stepmother and a neighbor earlier. "So I guess Henry will be going off to the military come fall," the neighbor said.

"Naw, I think Papa's decided to keep him here to run the farm." Even though he was her husband, Henry's stepmother called him Papa—just as the children did. It was no wonder. He was thirty some years her senior. Papa had outlived two wives already. The first one ten years his junior and the second one twenty, and they were sisters, not uncommon in Papa's day and not unheard of even now.

"I'm gonna' tell him, and this time, he's gonna' listen." Henry gave himself a pep talk and rehearsal—a dry run that would be forgotten the moment Papa fixed those steel gray eyes on him. *Does Papa think I'm gonna' waste my life on this hardscrabble farm forever?* Henry looked at his calloused hands; his brown forearms flexed like steel cable.

Papa shut the door of the Hudson and walked up to the front porch. His movements were fluid and effortless, and did not betray his age. He stopped and looked up at Henry, "Evening Son. What you got your face all balled up about?"

"Is it true?"

"Is what true Boy? And I'll advise you to remember who you're addressing!" Papa stepped onto the porch and looked down at Henry. Papa was six-feet plus, blinding white hair, broad shoulders and a huge handlebar mustache—impeccably groomed and dapperly dressed.

It was 95 degrees and Henry was shivering. He swallowed hard. "Is it true you want me to stay and work the farm instead of going into the Navy?"

"Yes Henry, that's exactly what I *need,* not *want,* you to do. I'm too busy at the bank and your little brother and sister are no help at all."

The bank. *Papa don't do shit at the bank, 'cept chew the rag and walk around town like a rich planter.*

Truth was Papa knew nothing about banking, and although well off, he was far from rich. The farm had turned a nice profit since The Reconstruction, but only because Papa was a frugal and innovative farmer. He came up with most of the seed money to get the bank started after Reconstruction. No one ever figured out where he got it. In return the bank gave him an office, a small monthly stipend and an exorbitant amount of interest on his original investment.

"Papa please. You can hire somebody to oversee the farm. You got plenty money."

"Boy, nobody's got plenty money now. We're in the middle of a depression. Nobody knows how I want this place run but you. It's your calling. Take the Hudson and go pick up your gal and take her for a ride." He tossed Henry the keys. "But mind you keep it out the ditches."

Henry couldn't believe he hadn't swallowed any number of insects, his mouth being open wide as a barn door and all. Nobody drove the Hudson but Papa.

"This land is in your blood. Our kin's been here for over a hundred years and here we'll stay. You're the best farmer of all my boys. Almost as good as your old Papa." He put his arm around Henry. "Smile boy. Go pick up your girl, but mind you don't let your blood boil too thick. Least not till you're married. Now go on and have a good time. Here." Papa dropped a twenty-dollar gold piece in Henry's hand, more money than most folks made in a month.

"Thank you, Papa."

"Just don't you forget, blood is blood, and everybody else is everybody else."

Henry got in the Hudson and drove down the dusty lane.

That's how Papa bought Henry's dreams, for a night in the Hudson and twenty dollars.

•••

SOUTHAMPTON COUNTY, VIRGINIA: 1976

Henry sat on a rough-hewn bench, the cold double circle of the shotgun barrel beneath his chin. The smokehouse was his Papa's spot—an 8x8 clubhouse where he drank, cussed and escaped the womenfolk.

Papa don't take no mess.

He adjusted the barrel just so, "Papa always said, squeeze the trigger gently." Henry did exactly what Papa said.

A murder of crows scattered into the purple twilight.

•••

NEW YORK CITY

The phone rang.

"Damn, what time is it?" The alarm clock read: 6:21A.M. *Who the hell is calling me this early?* He picked up the phone, "Hello."

"Sam?"

"Grandma?"

"I'm sorry to call so early baby, but I got some bad news."

"What's wrong Grandma?"

"I'm afraid there's been," she sighed, "an accident."

"What happened?"

"Your father… I'm sure it was an accident but…your daddy is dead."

"He's what?"

"Well… evidently, he was cleaning the shotgun… and I guess… he forgot to check and see if it was loaded and… well, it went off." Grandma wept.

Didn't know the gun was loaded. Daddy never picked up a gun in his life and not checked to see if it was loaded. Sam knew he should be all to pieces—in shock—or something.

"Grandma, I'll take the next train. I'll be there sometime late this afternoon. I'll call before I leave the station and tell you what time to send Zeke to pick me up."

"Alright baby, thank you."

"You don't have to thank me. I'll come home and take care of everything."

"Okay Sam."

"And Grandma…"

"Yes baby?"

"I love you."

"I love you too baby, goodbye."

"Bye Grandma."

The form under the bed sheet came to life. He had forgotten Cat was there. She sat up and rubbed her eyes. "Who was that?"

"My Grandma." He sat up.

"Is there something wrong?"

"Yeah…my daddy's dead." She hugged him. He felt her bare breasts on his back. Images flashed through his mind like black and white photographs. *Daddy…* "I've got to go home."

"Of course you do." She pulled her arms tighter around his neck and rubbed his head. "I'll help you pack and see you off."

"You don't have to do that, I'll be okay."

"I'll brew us some coffee and pack your suitcase. You should probably take a shower."

"Thank you baby."

He stood in the shower and felt the hot water scald him into consciousness. He needed to think. He had the next two weeks off, so he had plenty of time.

How are the boys taking it? Grandma was strong. *How old was she now?*

Sam's mother left them when he and his brothers were boys. Grandma had raised them. She was *still* raising his brothers.

Water ran down his lean body—his boyhood years on the farm had made him wiry and muscular. He dried off, wrapped a towel around his waist and went into the room. There was coffee on the nightstand and Cat was busy packing his things.

"How long are you going to be gone?" She was wearing a pair of black panties and one of his t-shirts. He walked up behind her and pressed himself against the smooth crevice of black silk.

"Umm… you're obviously not overcome with grief."

He dropped the towel, peeled the t-shirt over her head, moved her long dark hair aside and kissed her neck and shoulders. "I'm gonna' be gone at least a week, maybe two," he whispered in her ear, "I wanna' make sure I've got you burned into my memory."

"Okay, but you've got to talk to me on the ride to Penn Station and tell me about you and your dad."

"Sure," he whispered. She slid her underwear down her long legs. Sam entered her and felt alive. He was alive and Daddy was dead. He'd deal with that when he got home.

Cat was beautiful, intelligent, independent and a little crazy. Sam loved her. He never told her though, he couldn't. She was twenty-six. He was twenty-two and he knew, even though the age difference was small, he brought out the maternal instinct in her. She took care of him, and right now she thought the best way to do that was to get him to talk.

"So what's the story between you and your dad?"

"What? There's no story."

"Bullshit." She was right—it was bullshit. She knew him well. They had been seeing each other for months. There was no commitment between them, but they both wished the other would ask for one.

"Okay there is a story, and I'll tell it someday, but right now I gotta' see a man about a train." Riding with a NYC cabbie was something he had never gotten used to. When he first came to New York, he'd found the city exciting. Now it seemed alien, a huge beast designed to confuse, frighten and impede. They'd be at Penn Station in a moment and this uncomfortable interrogation would be over.

"I'm gonna' hold you to that when you get back." She smiled. Her big green eyes scrutinized his façade and penetrated his defenses.

"I'll tell ya' this much. Daddy was a great father." Though he was sugar coating he continued, "But we never became friends."

"So when did you say you'd be back?"

"A week and a half, two weeks tops." He knew she'd have plenty to do. She ran an art gallery and dealt with pretentious artists and their wealthy patrons.

"Call me when you get there."

"Sure baby, I'll miss you."

"Yeah, yeah, just take care of things back home and get your cute little ass back here ASAP!"

"Yes ma'am."

When the cab stopped, he kissed her—a short, desperate kiss that left him dazed. "Cat, I... I'll be thinking about you."

She shot him a puzzled look. "Yeah, me too."

"Bye."

"Goodbye, Sam."

He walked to the ticket counter. "One way to Suffolk, Virginia." That was as close as he could get to Southampton. Sam had an hour wait. He found a pay phone and let Grandma know what time to send Zeke to pick him up. Then he went to the nearest waiting area, fished the whiskey flask Cat packed for him out of his bag, took a long swig and then another.

Well Daddy, you got your way. I'm comin' home.

Sam slung his bag into the overhead compartment and sat down. *Daddy wasn't cleaning the gun. He killed himself.* As that seeped into his mind, he thought about what he had to do. Daddy had left the farm to Grandma. Sam was sure of it. He couldn't have left it to Sam's brothers. Daddy had made it clear how he felt about Lem and Zeke running the farm when Sam left…

Sam could still see the back of his daddy's head as he rocked in Papa's chair and spit the words out of his drunken mouth: "So you're gonna' run off and play music and have a high ol' time, while I try and run this farm with your brothers. Dem boys ain't right. Their backs are strong enough and we'll manage, but they cain't help me with any of the stuff you take care of… I'm gettin' old. This place is gonna' run to seed. Papa would turn over in his grave. But go on, I don't wanna' keep ya' from your hi-tone dreams…you're just like your mama, cut and run and ta' hell with the rest of us." The words hurt, but truth was Sam was just like his mama. And just like his mama he had sense enough to leave.

Sam walked to the club car, ordered a beer and a shot and sat down. It was 8:52 A.M. The bartender didn't raise an eyebrow. "That'll be three-seventy-five."

Sam gave him a five. "Keep it," he lit a smoke and thought of Cat…the kiss at Penn Station, the smell of her hair and the dimples just above her buttocks.

He downed his shot, ordered another and flipped it into the back of his throat. He walked back to his passenger seat, closed his eyes and tried to rest.

The train pulled into Union Station in D.C.

Sam was dreaming: laid out half-naked on his back under a baby-blue blanket of sky. *She* stood over him, brown legs, cut-off jeans, downy blond hair on her upper thighs, her breasts perfect, tan globes. She straddled him, kissed his chest, her tongue-teased his nipples: Serpentine…

After finishing his lunch, Sam stood on the platform and smoked.

The conductor shouted, "All aboard!"

It sounded romantic—in the movies.

He settled back into his seat. It was hard to concentrate. First the funeral, second the boys and Grandma, and then—back to his life; playing guitar and singing for a handful of rich drunks every night. At least he wasn't breaking his balls farming, working twelve to eighteen hour days, sweat glistening on his sunburned back, knotted muscles and calloused hands breaking sod and driving fence posts. He'd watched the land break his daddy. He was determined it wouldn't happen to him. He was determined when he left four years ago, and he was determined now.

Zeke drove down Route 58 towards Suffolk. He hummed an old blues tune that he'd heard Thaddeus play. Zeke had one thing on his mind: Sam. He missed his brother. Zeke was older than Sam, but he looked up to his younger brother. Daddy never had much patience with Zeke and Lem. He called them names, but never failed to put them to use around the farm. Zeke's particular talent was machines. He connected with gears and circuitry in an intuitive way. He'd cock his head to one side like a dog and hear the problem; his nerve endings and synapses received the data like a TV antenna. Daddy always said, "That boy is dumb as Carolina dirt, but damn if he ain't the wiz when it comes to machinery." Picking up Sam, despite the circumstances, made his heart pump like the pistons in a six-cylinder.

Sam could see the peanut mills of Suffolk silhouetted against the sky. The town smelled like peanuts and tricked you into believing you were entering a ballpark or boardwalk—the perfect summers' day. He stepped off the platform and looked for the truck. There it was, a baby blue, '67 Chevy pickup, weathered on the outside—mechanical symphony on the inside. *Damn, Zeke is good.*

"Sam!" Zeke walked towards his brother—arms stretched wide. "Sam," Zeke repeated as he hugged him and sobbed. He was a thirty year-old man frozen in childhood. It was pure and simple, just not practical.

"Zeke, buddy, don't squeeze so hard." Zeke was strong. "Put me down! I've missed you too man. Don't cry. Get in, I'll drive back."

Sam pumped Zeke for as much information as he dared. Zeke had stopped crying and Sam didn't want to release the floodgates again so he chose his words carefully.

"Were you home when Daddy, uhhhhh… had his accident?"

"Yeah, I found him."

"Zeke, I'm sorry man."

"Daddy was… he… his head was mostly gone… blood everywhere… I… I… couldn't fix him."

"*Nobody* could fix him at that point Zeke. Nobody could *ever* fix Daddy, not even Mama."

Zeke shot Sam a puzzled look. "Where *is* Mama?"

"I don't know Zeke, nobody knows."

"But she'll come home now. She'll have to. She'll have to 'cuz Daddy's dead," and then the crying started again.

"Zeke, don't cry. Mama left a long time ago. You know that. We only got that one letter from her, the one I read to you and Lem when we were kids, remember?"

"Yeah, I remember. Sam?"

"What Zeke?"

"I know why Mama left."

"She explained why in the letter Zeke."

"No, I know why she *really* left."

"Why Zeke?"

"She left 'cuz me and Lem are stupid." He said that so matter of fact that it made Sam angry.

"Don't you ever say that! Mama loved, I mean loves you and Lem. She loves all three of us. She always has. It was *him*. It was him she didn't love. It was Daddy she ran away from. I just wish she had been strong enough to take us with her." Then Sam began to cry, a steady leak, a cold constant flow of tears. *Why Mama?*

Sam drove through Franklin and headed into the country.

The long, flat, two-lane road stretched as far as he could see, tall pines on either side anchored firmly in the swampy earth. He was going back in time to a place where blacks still doffed their caps and said, 'Howdy Cap'n,' and white folks still spoke of, "The War Between the States," as if it were yesterday. He'd spent most of his boyhood dreaming of escaping this place and now he was returning on his own account, with a little help from Daddy. Zeke was speechless and had been for the most part since they'd left Suffolk.

Zeke broke the uncomfortable silence. "Sam?"

"Yeah Zeke."

"That girl stopped by yesterday."

"What girl Zeke?"

"The pretty one."

"The pretty one? What pretty one?"

"The one on the horse." *Well... that certainly narrowed it down.* Sometimes, talking to Zeke was an Abbott and Costello routine.

"What's her name Zeke?" he already knew but he wanted to hear Zeke say it.

"Ssss... Ssss... Summer."

"Oh yeah, what did she have to say?"

"She asked about how we wuz' doin' and talked to Grandma for awhile."

"That's nice," *and did she tell ya'll how she broke my heart?*

"But she really came by to see you."

"Ya' think so?"

"Yeah."

They rode on in silence and Sam replayed the last time he saw her...

It was prom weekend 1972 and like most kids from Southeastern Virginia they were spending the weekend on the Outer Banks of North Carolina. Summer and her friends stayed at the Riddick's cottage. Judge Riddick, Summer's dad, had had the place built in the early 50s. It was on the beach and calling it a cottage was an understatement. It was as spacious as the house Sam grew up in.

Sam and Summer spent the weekend partying, tanning, swimming and screwing. He was in love with her and she *said* she was with him, but Sam thought otherwise. He knew that she would always say what suited her purpose at the moment. One boy would never be enough for a girl like her.

They dated off and on all through high school: got drunk in the woods, skinny dipped in the river, smoked pot in the Judge's Cadillac, had sex on the back of a horse and tripped on acid together.

He'd never forget the last time they made love: the curve of her lower back slick with sweat, the smell of salt and sex, the white noise of the surf, hard brown flesh, a fistful of long blond hair as Sam thrust into her, deep, deeper. He wanted to possess her, to love her, to hurt her.

Just as they finished her oldest sister walked up. "What the fuck are you two doing?"

Summer pulled her bikini bottoms up and lit a cigarette. "Has it been that long Sis'? You should try it yourself sometime. Maybe you wouldn't be so fucking uptight." Sam looked at Virginia (Summer's sister) and mouthed, 'I'm sorry' and walked behind Summer towards the beach.

"Don't worry Sam. She won't tell Daddy." The Judge liked Sam and Sam him.

"Are you sure?"

"Yeah, I'm sure. I've got way better shit on her. Remember when I caught her in the stable giving head to that white trash bitch? She won't say a word. Daddy will always love you, even if I can't."

"What are you talking about?"

"Here, light this… we'll talk in a little while. Right now I wanna' walk down the beach and get high."

They walked and smoked…

Summer tossed the roach into the surf and said, "Look Sam, I do love you, but I'm going to Longwood in the fall and you're going… well, I don't know where you're going, but I'm sure it's somewhere a helluva' lot more exciting than college. There's no need to kid ourselves, and besides, I'm gonna' be here all summer and you're gonna' be back home helping your daddy on the farm."

He pulled her close and looked into her eyes. "I know. You're right. I don't know what I'm gonna' do. I've already pissed Daddy off by refusing to go to Tech and study agriculture."

"Don't waste your life on that dirt farm. You're a good guitar player and an amazing singer. Go play music… travel… live. I'd *kill* for your talent." Her fingertips traced his tan chest.

"Damn, I don't wanna' lose you."

"You'll never lose me. I'll always be your friend and I'll always love you." She stuck her hand in his swim trunks and gave him a squeeze. "And I'll always be willing to bend over and let you drive."

"Stop Summer, I gotta' go."

"Where? We don't have to leave till tomorrow."

"All of a sudden I'd rather be alone."

"You're gonna' miss one helluva party tonight. Well, whatever, suit yourself."

He turned and walked down the beach, and didn't look back.

He thought he'd see her at graduation. He didn't. Sam made up his mind. He'd go on the road and erase Summer from his memory.

Sam swung the old pickup to the right and started down the long dirt lane to the house. Nothing had changed. The old pecan trees stood guard as the truck kicked up a gray snake of dust. Sam could see Lem and Thaddeus on the porch waving as they approached. Thaddeus was an enormous black man of indeterminable age: mahogany skin, shoulders like cannonballs, hands as big as ham steaks and a tight salt and pepper afro topped by an old gray fedora. He could've been in his fifties. He could've been 80. Lem's face split into a grin as the truck rolled to a stop. Sam stepped out of the truck as Lem approached, arms outstretched.

"Damn, not again," Sam said as Lem picked him up in a viselike hug. "Shit, what the hell does Grandma feed you guys? You're both strong as an ox!"

"I'm sorry Sam. I miss you," Lem said.

Then it was Thad's turn. "I'll take pity on yo' po' skinny ribs Mr. Sam," Thad reached out and engulfed Sam's hand in his firm sand paper grip. It's good to see ya', how's the big city?"

"New York is New York, Thad."

"Yeah, I reckon it is. Come on in the house, and see yo' Grandma. She's been missin' ya' too."

Everybody wiped their feet before entering the house, Grandma's rules. She met them in the foyer, "Sam, Sam, I've missed you sooooooo much!" She threw her arm around him. She only had one. She'd been born that way. No one knew why. It didn't matter. Grandma could do more with one arm than most people could with two, and God help the man that didn't realize it.

Thad put on his hat. "Come on boys, we gots work to do. Sam needs some time to talk to your Grandma."

Sam watched through the kitchen window as Thad and his brothers walked off towards the barn, three gentle giants.

As Sam sat down, Grandma put a cup of coffee in front of him. He took a sip of the potent brew and whispered something his daddy used to say, "That woman makes a cup of coffee strong enough to slap a man into consciousness." Then louder, "Mmmmm… that's good Grandma. Now, tell me exactly what happened."

"He was in Papa's smokehouse. Drinkin' I 'spect, and the shotgun went off."

"Shotguns don't just go off Grandma. Did the sheriff come out here and investigate?"

"Well, I don't know how much investigating he did, but he did say sumpin' 'bout suicide. Silliest thing I ever heard. No son of Papa's would ever take his own life."

"Zeke told me he found Daddy."

"Yeah, poor thing. Zeke came in here stuttering and crying, blood all over him. Took me ten minutes to figure out what he was talkin' 'bout."

"Is there a copy of Daddy's will here?"

"Not that I know of son. Josh Pretlow down in Franklin's probably got the only copy."

"So, where is Daddy?"

"Well, they had to do an autopsy, which I don't understand. It just don't seem Christian, cuttin' a man up like that, but I think they moved him over to the funeral home sometime earlier today."

"So we need to go over and talk about the arrangements, huh?"

"Yeah Sam, tomorrow I reckon."

Sam got up and kissed Grandma on the top of her head. "I'm gonna' go walk the property and see how things are around here and talk to Thaddeus for a few minutes."

"Okay. Sam?"

"Yeah, I know Grandma, supper at 5:30 sharp."

"That's my boy. See ya' then."

"Okay Grandma."

Sam walked across the backyard to the barn. He peeked around the side of the open door and saw Lem talking to one of the two milking cows they still kept. Most folks bought their cheese, butter and milk at the A&P in Franklin—not Grandma. Lem milked the cow and sang: "Woke up this mawning, and my baby was gone, lawdy lawdy lawdy, lawd have mercy on me." Lem's voice hung in the air like molasses and soothed every living thing within earshot. *Damn, he sounds like Mama.*

Sam left Lem with the cow. The two of them seemed content. He walked the perimeter of the back field to the woods line, then down beside the tall pines into the orchard of apple and peach trees past the fig bushes and scuppernong vine and back up to the out buildings between the peanut fields.

Opening the smokehouse door Sam saw the wooden bench Daddy used to sit on, the same one Papa used to sit on, the one Papa's father had made before the Civil War...

Sam looked at the red hams hanging, swinging. He smelled

the damp earth and the salt. Sun split cracks; shafts of light lit a liquor bottle, the shotgun and blood.

Sam felt his stomach flip-flop and he left the smokehouse.

Outside, he took a few gulps of air and lit a cigarette. Across the grassy lane, he saw Thaddeus and Zeke under the old tractor shed, tinkering with a geriatric generator. Machinery was a mystery to Sam.

Zeke adjusted something, his hands moved but he stared into space, tongue out, calm and intent. Sam gestured to Thad and they slipped away.

"I don't know how dat boy does it," said Thad.

"None of us ever did."

"He don't even look at it. He hears it, and then he feels it through his hands. 'Minds me of an old tent preacher used to come through here years ago. He could lay hands on folks and fix 'em."

"Yeah, Thad I know the story… Look, Daddy and you were best friends. He told you everything. How are things around here?"

"Well, I don't know how much you know 'bout what's been going on around here, but your daddy and dis here place were in a little trouble."

"How much little trouble Thad? Give it to me straight."

"Okay, the bank calls your daddy twice a month or more. I know he's at least two months behind on the tractor loan. He owes back property taxes, how much he never told me. He was always prideful to a fault, that man. I also know fo' sho' he's way behind on the feed, seed, fertilizer and pesticide bill. I know that cuz I went up to the feed and seed to put some stuff on account yesterday and they wouldn't extend your daddy's credit. I 'spect you'll find out more when you go see da lawyer 'bout your daddy's will. Lately Sam your Daddy had just commenced to acting strange… and looking scared." Thad took off his hat, wiped his brow and looked across the field towards the woods.

"Thad… Thad… what do you think? Can the farm be saved?"

Thaddeus looked at Sam, "Yeah… but it'll take a lot of hard

work and somebody with a head and heart for farming."

"Daddy left the place to Grandma. So, most likely, she'll rent the land to either the Drakes or the Grays and use the money to get caught up."

"Maybe."

"What do you mean maybe? Do you know something I don't?"

"No, not me, Mistah Sam, I don't know nuttin. I'm just a ignant colored farm hand."

"Don't give me that Uncle Tom shit. You've always been way more than a hand around here and you're not colored anymore, you're Negro… or black… or something. You need to get out of this county more often. Anyway, I'll find out tomorrow, when I go see the lawyer. I gotta' make a phone call."

"Ya wouldn't be callin' a gal now would ya?"

"As a matter of fact, I am."

"She must be sumpin."

"Why you say that?"

"Cuz if you're callin' all the way up to New York while you going through all dis, she *got to be* sumpin. You love her?"

"Damn, you're nosier than Grandma. But as a matter of fact, I do love her." *Damn, that's the first time I ever said that.*

Sam heard her first…and then, there she was, coming across the field at a full gallop, backlit, grand sunset entrance on a midnight stallion.

Sam knew who it was immediately. Even in silhouette, he knew. She stopped the muscular horse a few feet in front of Thad and Sam.

"Lawd have mercy." Thaddeus shook his head and smiled.

She took off her riding cap and shook out her long blond hair. She wore tight black riding pants and a frilly white blouse that revealed just a hint of cleavage. Sam's breath quickened, beads of perspiration trickled from his armpits and down his rib cage.

"Hey Sam," she said as she slid from the horse and came to him. She kissed him on the cheek and her body molded around his. Suddenly uncomfortable, he pulled away.

"Hello Thaddeus," she said with ease.

"How do Miss Summer," Thad tipped his hat. "You two have a nice day. I gots work to do 'fore sundown. Looks to me like you got some thinkin' to do boy." Thad said the last part so only Sam could hear and walked off.

Thad hadn't taken that tone with Sam since he was a boy.

Sam sat down, Summer sat in his lap. She massaged his back and shoulders with one hand while she nuzzled him and rubbed his chest with the other.

"Are you okay?" she smelled dark and musky, a combination of her scent and the horse's.

"Yeah Summer, I'm okay."

"I'm sorry about your dad."

"Yeah, so am I."

"Do you wanna' talk about it?"

"There's nothing to talk about."

"Okay, well, do you wanna' talk about anything else, like maybe, us?"

"What us? Summer, there never was an us. You made that clear in Nags Head four years ago."

"You're right, I did, and I thought you understood."

"Understood what? That you didn't want to be with me? That you couldn't love a guy like me? That I would never be enough for you? That your mama thought I was poor white trash? I knew *she* thought that, but I never knew you did!"

"What are you talking about? Daddy always loved you. Mama… Mama's just Mama."

"Okay Summer, none of that matters right now, I got bigger fish to fry."

"Yeah I know you got a lotta' things on you right now, but I want you to know I'm here for you."

I'm sure you are, your body anyway, but what about the rest of you?

"How about I come around late tonight and we have a couple drinks just like old times." She squeezed his arm and added, "I've missed you."

I never could say no to her. "Alright Summer, I could probably use the company. What time?"

"Around eleven, I have a dinner party to attend and then I'll ride over and we'll hang out." She grabbed his hair and kissed him —hard. He felt the blood rush to his loins and she squirmed a little in his lap, stood and mounted the masculine ebony beast and galloped off.

Sam shook his head. "I don't need this right now. Summer… fuckin' Summer Riddick." He walked towards the house to make his phone call and hoped he had enough blood left in his brain to carry on a conversation.

Sam sat on the front porch and strummed his guitar. It was eleven o'clock and there was no sign of Summer—yet. Playing the old acoustic always made him feel like he was floating down the river on a raft, lying on his back in the hot sun, a vast expanse of blue sky in a green canopy frame, a wet breeze on bare flesh, weightless, directionless, belonging to everything and nothing at all.

He wasn't much of a lead player, but his rhythm was fluid and seamless. Liquid Smoke. He looked up at the huge yellow moon.

Damn, it would have to be full.

He heard the hooves as they beat a fast pattern on the ground behind him.

Shit, she's comin' through the woods.

The old trail from Judge Riddick's place through Papa's woods was dangerous in the daylight but to attempt it at night, even for an experienced rider, was foolish. Sam calmed down as he heard the horse slow to a trot. He walked around the house to meet her. She was halfway down the grassy strip between the fields, and this time she was lit from the front.

The moon cast a spotlight on her that she worked like a pro, her hair ribbons of glass, she had on a black chemise and tight jeans. Sam's breath caught as she threw a leg over and slid off the huge horse with a drunken elegance he couldn't help but admire.

"Damn, you're beautiful." *Did I say that out loud?* He hadn't meant to.

"Why thank you, you're pretty damn cute yourself." She pulled a bottle of Moet from the saddlebag. "Compliments of the Judge."

"Come on, let's put the horse in the barn and get him some feed and water," Sam said and they turned and walked towards the barn. Summer smacked Sam's rear with her riding crop. "Oww!"

"Oh shut up, you liked it." He did. He didn't know why he *did* and he wasn't sure he wanted to know why he *did,* but he *did.*

They stalled the horse and saw to its feed and water. Summer said, "Let's go up to the loft and smoke this," she held up a joint and grinned, proud of herself.

Climbing up to the loft Sam felt a pang of guilt. He knew where this was headed and he couldn't stop it. There was no spoken commitment between he and Cat but this was wrong.

Summer fell into a pile of hay and asked for a light. They lay in the hay smoking. Silent.

Finally, Summer sat up and whispered, "I've missed you."

"Oh yeah, you coulda' fooled me."

"I've never fooled you. You're the most perceptive and intelligent man I've ever known, with the possible exception of my daddy."

"Then why wasn't I ever enough for you? Why did you always have to have: the football star, the rich boy, the new boy, the nerd, the black guy, the European exchange student… the list goes on and on."

"You had your little side sluts. I wasn't the only one."

"I did what I did because of what you kept doing. I didn't want anybody but you. You knew that!"

"Look, can we be nice tonight? I said what I said at the beach that day because I was going to college, you were going on the road or whatever, and I thought it was best for both of us. I've always loved you and you know that." She straddled him and ripped open his shirt sending buttons flying all over the loft.

She popped the cork on the champagne like a seasoned somme-lier and it overflowed, running down his torso in tiny rivers. She licked it up and raked her nails down his sides—crimson stripes —his flesh marked. He wrapped her hair around his fist and pulled her down. He wanted her to devour him, until there was nothing left.

They stood in front of the barn and smoked cigarettes.

"We can't do this."

"We can't do what Sam?"

"This," he pointed to the loft, "that."

"Why not? We love each other and right now we need each other."

"Don't you have a boyfriend or something?"

"Lots of boys, no friends."

"Well I've got a girlfriend." *Do I?*

"Well that's funny. I don't remember you mentioning her while you were in my mouth."

"That doesn't matter! I'm mentioning her now."

"Yeah, I hear ya' Sam. Get a good night's sleep, you're gonna' need it. I'll see ya' tomorrow. You can let me know then if you need help with anything."

Sam was speechless. Summer went to fetch the horse. She walked back out with her stallion in tow. She grabbed Sam by his torn shirt and pulled him to her, kissed and then, "Shit!" bit him. "What the fuck did you do that for?"

"We play rough Sam, we always did."

"Not anymore Summer. *We* can't play anymore. *You* can't play with *me* anymore."

"Who said I'm playing this time? I'll see ya' tomorrow." She mounted her horse and galloped off.

"I gotta' give it to her. She sure as hell knows how to make an exit."

Sam climbed the stairs to his old room and fell backwards onto the bed. He stared at the ceiling. His room was just as he had left it, with the exception of a thorough cleaning, most likely done by Lem or Zeke at Grandma's instruction. He scanned the posters of various rock bands he had tacked to the walls: Jimmy Page, Robert Plant, Pete Townsend and Roger Daltrey. All of them stared at him with disdain. They spoke to him, their condescending English accents echoing in his head: "We knew you'd be back bloke, no stupid American hillbilly could possibly have what it takes to be one of us." *What is wrong with me?*

I've just had my brains fucked out by Summer Riddick—the most poisonous bitch of all time and now… now the posters in my room are talking to me, and yeah, oh yeah, tomorrow I've got to go and make funeral arrangements for my dad. What else? What next?

The phone rang.

There was no extension in his room.

Mr. Big Shot New York City Musician gets a phone call and now everybody in the house is awake. It was after midnight. He knew it was for him.

"Sam," he heard his grandma call up the stairs, "telephone."

Sam was already halfway down the staircase. "Sorry Grandma. Thanks, goodnight." He tiptoed into the kitchen and picked up the phone.

"Hello."

"Yo Sam, its Ricky."

"Ricky, what the fuck are you doing calling me at this hour?"

"Dude, it's only a little after twelve."

"That's early in New York man, but down here it's late, damn late."

"Sorry Sam, look, I got the number from Cat. I didn't think you'd mind and she seemed to think you'd want to hear this right away."

"What Ricky? What?" Sam hissed, trying to be quiet.

"You remember that demo we cut right before we took the house gig in New York?"

"That funk rock tune? The one we wrote in Indianapolis?"

"Yeah, it just so happens the engineer that cut the demo for us in that shitty little studio in Richmond just got a job working for some big time producer at Capitol Records. He let this fat cat producer hear the demo and the guy went ape-shit over it. They want to talk contract man, fucking contract!"

Great. Talk about bad timing. Things couldn't get any worse. Sam had wanted this since he was twelve years old and now that it had just fallen into his lap all he could think about was how much of an inconvenience it was.

"Ricky, I can't deal with this right now. I gotta' bury my dad day after tomorrow."

"Oh yeah…man, I'm sorry. But I need to know when you'll be back. We gotta' rehearse and write some songs."

"Shit, it'll be a week or more before I can get back up there."

"Yeah, that's what Cat said. We're gonna' start writing tomorrow, so the sooner the better."

"Yeah, I get that Ricky. I'll call ya' at the end of the week, bye." He hung up.

When Sam and his grandma entered the Victorian funeral home the next morning, Sam's head was ringing like a bell clapper. He wasn't sure if it was from last night's Champagne and weed, or the stench of embalming fluid. Silas Stone greeted them in the foyer. Silas was the stereotypical mortician: tall, gaunt, hollow cheeked and solemn. When Sam was a kid, he and his friends called Silas the "grim reaper." He shook Sam's hand. Silas's long bony palm and fingers felt like a fistful of dead herrings.

"Good morning Sam, Mrs. Thomas." Silas spoke in a whisper, as if anything louder would literally wake the dead. "Right this way," he lisped.

Geez', maybe we should be burying Silas instead of Daddy.

They entered Silas's office and began their discussion. Sam took charge right away, "We want everything short and simple. Simple casket, short service—wake at the house afterwards."

"Open or closed casket?" Silas asked.

"Closed," Sam said.

Grandma took it from there and handled the details: casket color and style, two hymns for the service, Reverend Williams with the eulogy and done. *Daddy in a box. In the ground. Done.*

They left the funeral home and walked across the street to

the lawyer's office.

"That was reasonably painless," Sam said.

"What son?"

"Nothing Grandma, nothing."

"Let's go see what Joshua has to say."

"Yeah, lets."

The secretary greeted them and sent them right in.

Joshua Pretlow peered over his bifocals, uncrossed his legs, stood up and said, "Good morning. I'm so sorry about your daddy Sam. Hello Mrs. Thomas." He gave Grandma a hug. "So… your daddy's will was short and simple. You want me to read it verbatim or just give you the gist?" Joshua straightened his tie and cleared his throat.

"Just the bottom line," Sam wanted to get this over with.

"I can sum it up in one sentence. He left everything to you Sam." Joshua smiled, thinking he had just delivered good news.

"What!?"

"The house, the land, and what little was in the bank, it's all yours."

"What about Grandma and the boys? I don't want anything!" *Except my life!* He needed a drink.

"Sam, are you alright?" Grandma asked.

"Yeah Grandma, it's just I was hoping Daddy had left everything to you."

"Why? Papa left me well enough off. Your daddy wanted the house and farm to stay in the family, so he left it to you."

"Okay Josh, fine, we've got to go. Come on Grandma."

"Stop by one day next week Sam and I'll have the paperwork ready for you to sign and we can discuss things further after you've had some time to think." He placed the will back on his desk and moved his stapler and tape dispenser just so, a meticulous man. Sam's dad always called Joshua a "dandy."

"Thanks Josh." Sam got up and headed for the door.

"Thank you Joshua," Grandma said. She walked behind Sam towards the exit, then stopped and looked back, "We'll see you at the funeral day after tomorrow?"

"Or the wake, I may be in court during the funeral."

"Alright we'll see ya' then."

Sam stepped onto the sidewalk and lit a smoke.

Grandma gave him a sideways glance and said, "Those things'll kill ya' son."

"This trip home is killing me—cigarettes are an acceptable risk."

"What does that *mean* Son? Your mama use to say things like that. I never did understand that woman."

She never understood you either Grandma... or Daddy, or this place. He had to talk to Cat and Thad.

The phone rang at Cat's gallery. She answered it, "Gotham Art."

"Hello Gotham Art," Sam replied.

"Hey Sam! How are things going down there?"

Cat's voice calmed him but he still needed to vent. "Oh, couldn't be better. Where should I start? An old girlfriend is stalking me, a psycho one I might add. Ricky called in the middle of the night to tell me my dream had come true and I told him I had to finish living this nightmare first. Even as we speak, my daddy is being embalmed by a dead man. The posters in my room talk to me at night. I just inherited a farm that's up to its hayloft in debt and oh yeah, Grandma thinks smoking's gonna' kill me." He took a long swig from his whiskey flask.

"I think smoking is the least of your worries. When's the funeral?"

"Day after tomorrow."

"I'm coming down there. You don't sound so good."

"No Cat. You don't have to do that. You've got a business to run."

"That's why I have a competent assistant that's very well paid. Besides, I've been wanting to scout some folk artists in that area. That's going to be very big in the next few years and I want to get in on the ground floor. So who's the old girlfriend?"

"Oh, just somebody from high school," *and last night.* "Her name's Summer. Summer Riddick."

"Is she beautiful?"

"She's pretty, but she's also pretty crazy."

"Well, you tell her I'm on my way down there and I'm crazy too, except I'm New York City crazy and that beats the shit out of country crazy any day."

Shit, is this a good idea?

"Cat, you don't have to do this. I'll get through this on my own."

"I'll be on the red eye. You've got some decisions to make and I want to be there for you, and besides I need to protect you from psycho woman. I'll call you tonight and let you know when I'll be in Norfolk. You can pick me up, right?"

"Oh, yeah Cat sure, but you really don't have to do this."

"Shut up Sam, and Sam…"

"Yes babe?"

"I love you," she said, then hung up.

Sam stared at the phone. *I love you too.*

After supper, Sam sat on the front porch, strummed his guitar and sang a blues tune. One so old he wasn't sure who wrote it. He didn't care. When he sang it, it was his.

He heard a harmonica in the distance, in key and time with his guitar. *Thaddeus.* Thad walked around the corner of the house singing the second chorus in perfect harmony with Sam—voices that dovetailed like antique furniture. Flawless…

They ended the song. Sam lit a cigarette.

"You look like you could use a drink." Thaddeus held up a Mason jar of moonshine.

"Thad you were reading my mind." Sam took a long swig from the jar. "I'd know that shine anywhere, best in the state."

"Shit, best in the country, and you'd never know where I got the learning to make it."

"Where? Your daddy?"

"No, from your granddaddy, Papa."

"Papa? To hear everybody else tell it, Papa was a saint. Shit, to hear Grandma and Daddy tell it he could walk on water, a gen-u-wine miracle man."

"You'll never hear me dispute it. Besides, my mama never would tell me who my daddy was. All she'd ever do was get upset and tell me I was better off not knowin'."

"Don't get me started about my mama. My daddy, on the other hand, has just painted me in a corner for sure."

"Sam, you shouldn't be so hard on yo' daddy. He did the best he could raisin' you three on his own and I'm sure yo' mama had good reasons fo' doing what she did, although for the life of me I don't know what dey is. But den agin I never was much on the mysterious ways of white folks."

"So Papa made shine…"

"Now don't you go tellin' dis', but Papa did a lotta' shit folks don't know 'bout. He made and sold shine during prohibition, das' one of the reasons he had money when mos' folks didn't. He raised eleven chillun and kept the farm when a lotta' people had nuttin'."

"I know Thad. I've heard the legend of Papa."

"Yeah, but you didn't *know* the man. I did. He always did right by his blood; hell he always did right by me too. Don't go judgin' folks so hard, most of what you heard 'bout Papa came from your daddy and Grandma. Your grandma building him up, and your daddy tearing him down, da truth is somewhere in da middle. And your daddy, yeah, he had it hard livin' in Papa's shadow, but he brought a lot of it on himself too, lettin' Papa git to him like dat. I know you feel like you're bein' trapped, but your daddy gave you dis place because he loved you and he wanted dis place to stay in da family. He didn't do this to kill your dreams. He did it because it was all he ever knew. You know your daddy didn't wanna' stay here and run dis farm either. He wanted to go in the military and see the world. He used to talk my ears off 'bout exotic ports o' call. He had dreams too, just like you."

"Then why did he let Papa and this place beat him?"

"Boy, nobody beat yo' daddy. Not Papa. Not this place. Not life itself. He did the right thang and now you gotta' do the right thang." Thad set down the jar in front of Sam.

"I'm leavin' the jar, I 'spect you need it worse than I do."

Slowly, then, Thaddeus headed off, towards his house on the other side of the woods. Sam listened as the notes of Thad's harp faded on the breeze.

Sam took another long swig from the jar, screwed the lid back on, walked over to the truck, and hid it under the seat. Grandma abhorred drinking unless it was for medicinal purposes like her rheumatism. He sat back down on the porch and lit a smoke; at least, Summer hadn't popped up yet today. But Thad was right. Sam had a decision to make and he had to make it fast. Cat loved him. He had to figure out a way to keep Summer away from him and Cat until they went back to New York. That wasn't going to be easy. Summer was stubborn and devious when she wanted to be; what was she up to anyway? What did she mean by, 'Who said I'm playing this time?' She was always playing: the damsel in distress, the poor little rich girl, the seductress, the liberated woman.

Sam heard tires screeching at the end of the lane. It was Summer and she was in a brand new Corvette. She did a donut in the yard, stopped, killed the engine and got out.

"Sam, what's all the commotion?" Grandma was standing on the porch behind him.

"Nothing Grandma, just Summer."

It was hot for late April and Summer was obviously taking advantage of it; she walked up to the porch, all hips and attitude: cut-off jeans, bikini top, golden skin, legs up to her jawbone, man's ruin.

Under her breath, Grandma hissed, "Trollop," and then louder, "Hello Summer. Good to see you this evening."

"Hey Grandma, excuse my appearance. I took advantage of this warm weather to lay out and get a little color this afternoon. Hey Sam." She kissed him on the cheek and then hugged Grandma. Grandma went back inside mumbling to herself and shaking her head.

Sam grabbed Summer by the hand and led her to the smokehouse, "We've got to talk," he said as he pushed her inside.

She put her hand on his crotch and asked, "Talk, or fuck?"

"Talk Summer, there'll be no more fucking, that's over."

"It's never over between us Sam. You know that, and besides, this time it's different. It's not just your body I want. I want you, all of you. We belong together, I realized that the moment I saw you yesterday. I love you. You're home to stay now. I heard all about it. The farm is all yours and you've got to stay and take care of Lem and Zeke and Grandma. I know you. You can't run away from this, not this time."

"I don't know what I'm gonna' do yet, but that's beside the point. I love someone else and she'll be here tonight. So Summer, you need to leave me alone. You don't really want me anyway. I'm just a diversion, something to do until you lose interest and find someone else to do."

"Don't fuck with me Sam! I'm accustomed to getting what I want. You love me, you always have and now I'm ready to love you back, just you, and nobody else. I swear it'll be different this time. I'm not going anywhere. I can help you here on the farm, and besides you're gonna' need money. Everybody knows this place is in trouble. You're gonna' need a lot of money and when I get my trust fund, I'll have plenty." She reached into her cut-offs and took out a small plastic dish, unscrewed the lid, stuck her fingernail in it, lifted it to her nose and sniffed.

"So you're doing coke now? That's just great Summer! No wonder you're so fucking crazy. I want you to stay away from here, you understand me? I've got enough problems and I don't need your crazy ass adding to them."

Sam walked through the smokehouse door with Summer in hot pursuit. "Don't you walk away from me Samuel Lee Thomas! This isn't over, not by a long shot. I'll be at the funeral day after tomorrow, and at the wake after that, and maybe I'll tell your little Yankee bitch girlfriend how you fucked me in the mouth last night and neglected to tell me about her until I swallowed your cum and licked you clean, you motherfucker!"

"Very lady-like Summer. You kiss your mama with that mouth?"

"Fuck you Sam! You think you've got problems now. Just

wait, just you fucking wait!" She jumped in the 'vette and fish-tailed out of the yard, down the lane and onto the road, gone.

Sam stood there and shook his head. *She's gonna' be a problem, a big problem.*

Sam sat on the front porch smoking, smoking and thinking. Should he tell Cat everything? Just in case Summer made good on her threat. Or... should he just keep his mouth shut and hope for the best? Cat loved him. She had said so and she'd be here tonight. It was ten o'clock. Maybe he should lie down for a couple hours before he had to drive to Norfolk and pick her up. He walked into the house, started up the stairs and the phone rang.

"Hello."

"Damn, you have a sexy voice."

"Thank you, but I don't feel so sexy right now."

"That's okay; I'll take care of that in a few hours. I'm leaving a little after midnight. I'll be there at one-forty. You should probably get a couple hours sleep before you leave to pick me up."

"As usual, you're reading my mind. I was just getting ready to do that."

"Good, I need you rested and energized. I have to go pack."

"Okay baby, I'll see ya' at one-forty, and baby..."

"Yes Sam?"

"I love you."

Sam hung up before she could reply.

Sam pulled into the airport parking lot, got out and headed for the terminal. He lit a cigarette and decided he would tell her, he would tell Cat that he had sex with Summer the night before. *What the hell, Summer's gonna' tell her anyway. Why not beat her to the punch?* There was no commitment between him and Cat when it happened, no spoken words of love. At least, this way, he'd get to put his spin on it and Cat wouldn't be completely ambushed by Summer at the wake. That's what he would do, damage control. Lying would only make it worse.

She walked down the long corridor towards Sam. He spotted her from forty yards: confident stride, thousand watt eyes.

His circuitry sizzled, all of it, above and below the waist. Cat was perfect, even in faded jeans and t-shirt, especially in faded jeans and t-shirt and she belonged to him.

"Hey baby."

"Sam."

They hugged, no words, just contact, complete contact, like two people that had just come to a simultaneous revelation.

"How was your flight?"

"Fine, how are you holding up?"

"I'm okay; let's go get your bags."

Once Sam got the old pickup onto the highway and into fourth gear, he grabbed her hand and glanced at her. "What you said on the phone yesterday, when you said I love you..."

"Stop Sam. I said it because I felt it; I've been feeling it for quite sometime. I didn't say it for you to feel obligated to say it back. I said it because I wanted you to know that it is. And not saying it would be lying and we've always been honest with each other. In fact, I've got some other things I need to tell you, but they can wait. Why did *you* say it tonight and then hang up before I could say it back?"

"Because I was afraid I had imagined it, like it was a dream or something, and if you said it again, I'd wake up. So I said it tonight and hung up before you could tell me I was crazy and had imagined it all. I had to say it. I've felt it for awhile too, and I've also got something else to tell you."

"I love you Sam."

"I love you too Cat."

They rode the rest of the way to what was now Sam's house in silence, sipping shine, radio low, her head on his shoulder, rhythm and blues cruisin'; there was no need for words.

When they pulled in front of the house, Cat got out, looked at the battered pickup, smiled and said, "Nice truck."

"Thanks, Zeke keeps it runnin' like a champ." He grabbed her bags. "Thanks for packin' light," he groaned and set them down, readjusted his grip and said, "Right this way."

"So how long you staying?"

"As long as you need me to."

"Well, that's one of the things I need to talk to you about. It may be quite some time before I can leave."

"We can talk about it tomorrow. It's late now. What's the sleeping arrangement?"

"I'll tell ya' at the top of the stairs. Shhhhhhhhhhh…" they tiptoed up and tried not to giggle. They went down the length of the hall and into one of the guest rooms. Sam closed the door behind them and set the bags down.

"So this is my room?"

"No this is our room for a couple hours and then you sneak down the hall and sleep in my room. Then you have to get up around five and come back down here and sleep till breakfast, so my nosy ass brothers don't tell Grandma anything that will make her think less of you."

"What would Grandma think about all this deception?"

"Grandma's old and doesn't climb stairs, so what she don't know won't hurt her. But there is one problem; we have to make sure this bed looks slept in."

"Why? I thought Grandma didn't come up here."

"She doesn't, but my brothers do and they tell Grandma everything."

"Oh, okay. But I don't think making this bed look slept in is going to be any problem. As a matter of fact, I think it's going to be a pleasure."

They peeled each other's clothes off quickly, quietly, and with a sense of urgency and purpose. They kissed and tasted each other, all mouths and tongues and hands and raw nerve endings. Cat lowered herself onto Sam, slowly, her moans stifled, his pillow bit and, in a matter of minutes the bed looked slept in.

"Sam?" Grandma called up the steps, "You and your friend gonna' sleep the day away?"

It was nine o'clock in the morning. Sam sat up and shook the sleep from his head; the moonshine haze would be another matter entirely.

"Okay Grandma. We'll be down in a minute." He knew it

had killed her to let them sleep the two extra hours since breakfast. Grandma always had breakfast on the table at 7:00 A.M. sharp. Sam crept down the hall and into the guest room. He sat on the edge of the bed and watched Cat sleep. Her shiny ebony hair fanned out on the pillow like black silk. He caressed the spot on her lower spine just above her buttocks, then the sweet curve in the small of her back, and he kissed her there, tasting the salty musk of their sex the night before. He continued kissing all the way up her spine to her shoulders, she stirred.

"Mmmmmmm... Sam."

"Yeah baby?"

"Don't stop."

"I'd like nothing better than to stay in bed with you all day and explore every inch, crack and crevice of your sexy body with my tongue, but Grandma's expecting us downstairs for breakfast any minute."

She rolled over and parted her legs, "Kiss me here." And he did: kissed, licked, in a couple minutes she arched her back, and bit her hand while she came. Sam kissed her and stood up.

"Tasty, but not very filling, let's go have a big country breakfast."

"Sounds good. I'm starved," Cat agreed.

Grandma and Cat got along at breakfast as if they had known each other for years. Cat even helped Grandma clear the table and wash the dishes; something Grandma rarely let anyone do. After they were done with the dishes, Sam took Cat out to show her around the farm. They stopped first at a small goat pen where Lem was feeding and talking to a new kid.

"Hey Lem, come here. I want you to meet somebody."

"Hey Sam, who's that?"

"This is my girlfriend, Cat."

"She's purty." Lem beamed.

Cat smiled and said, "Why thank you Lem, it's nice to meet you," she extended her hand.

Lem went one better and held his arms out wide, inviting a hug.

"He wants to hug you," Sam said.

Cat leaned over the fence and allowed Lem to embrace her.

"Easy big fella, she's a girl," Sam said.

"She's purty, like Mama."

"Shit Lem, not you too. Mama's gone, she's been gone. She left us... you, Zeke, and me. She left cuz' of Daddy, and she ain't never coming back."

"Zeke said she was. He said she'd have to now on account of Daddy being dead. He said..."

"I don't care what Zeke said! He's a fool for saying it, and you're a bigger fool for listening to it, and I don't wanna' hear another fucking word about it outta' either one of ya'll!"

"Okay Sam. I'm sorry." Lem began to cry.

Cat stepped over the low fence and held Lem. "Shhhhh-hhh... Sam didn't mean it. All three of you miss your mom and your dad, and you are all upset right now, that's all."

Lem let go of Cat and said, "You wanna' see my baby?"

"Yes Lem, I'd love to see your baby," Cat replied.

Lem picked up the wobbly-kneed goat kid and held him like an infant.

"Look at this Sam, the way he talks to it. It's like it listens and understands."

"Yeah I know, I've seen it, he's a regular fucking Dr. Doolittle."

Sam stomped off a few yards but then stopped to look back.

Cat kissed the kid, Lem and then stepped over the fence. She looked as though she had always been there, as much a part of the landscape as Lem and the goats. She turned towards the pen and said, "Everything's going to be okay Lem. We'll see ya' later." She waved to Lem before catching up with Sam. "Why did you do that?"

"Do what?"

"Talk to him like that! He's hurting too. This isn't just about you."

"Yeah, but I'm the one all this has just fallen on. He left me everything, the house, the farm, my brothers. Such as it all is."

"What do you mean 'such as it is'? This is a beautiful place, most people would be thrilled to own a farm like this."

"Oh yeah? Would they be so thrilled when they found out it was up to the tops of its pecan trees in hock?" Sam's mood darkened. "Would they love it so much after they'd spent eighteen hours a day, sweating in the sun, just to squeeze enough out of it to keep it, huh? Would they love it so fucking much then?"

Cat took a deep breath and released it slowly. "All I know is you have a sweet brother and you just missed a beautiful moment right in your own backyard. Look at him Sam. Look at how he is with those goats. It's uncanny. You can feel the love between them."

"I know Cat. I love my brothers, and I also have a love/hate relationship with this farm, but you don't know what it was like. When I hear them talkin' that shit about Mama... her comin' home, you didn't see what it put them through. Hell, what it put me through, but I had to be strong for them because I was the normal one. I was the smart and mature one, but I was a little boy too. I didn't understand why she left either. I mean, now I do, at least some, because I know how much I felt like I had to leave this place. But how could she leave us with *him*? How could she leave *me* with *him*? All Daddy ever did was blame us for her leaving, Lem and Zeke mostly, cuz', well, you know how they are."

"No Sam I don't know. How are they? I haven't met Zeke yet, but all I saw back there was a good man, a kind and gentle man that loves animals and is good at what he does. That *is* what he *does* around here isn't it?"

"Yeah, for the most part. I just don't want 'em to get hurt again, not like that. We've gotten one lousy letter from her, one lousy letter in fifteen fucking years Cat." The ambivalent feelings Sam felt towards his mother rose in the back of his throat. "I've only read it once and I still remember every word, every word. And the worst thing is, now that I'm older, I understand some of it, I can relate to it, but she *ain't* comin' back, and I won't let them get their hopes up that she will."

Cat shot Sam a look of dismay. "Why didn't you ever tell me about all this? Why didn't you ever talk to me?"

"I don't remember you ever doing true family confessions with me, so I just figured that it was a can o' tuna neither one of us wanted to open up and sniff."

Cat walked up to Sam and put her arms around his neck, "Well, things are different now. I'm your girlfriend, right?"

"Yeah, as a matter of fact you are."

She kissed him tenderly. Then they walked in silence for a while, holding hands, and for the first time since he was a child, Sam felt like he was home.

Cat broke the silence first, "You know, my childhood wasn't exactly perfect Sam. I grew up on a large estate in Connecticut: horses, dogs, cats, tons of land and a huge house. But I can relate to what you went through, at least some of it. My mom left when I was ten. She ran off with the gardener. Yeah, I know. It's the subject of bad romance novels and TV movies, but it actually happens." They stopped at the end of the grassy strip between the fields and sat on an old tree stump. "My dad never talked about it. My nanny explained it to me and not very well I might add. My dad's in publishing, our family has been for many years, so he was always in New York or traveling. He tried his best with me when he was at home, but I always got the impression he'd rather be in his study, sitting in his leather bound chair, surrounded by his rare books and sipping brandy. You know, I've never once seen him angry, or passionate for that matter, about anything. But I always knew he loved me." Cat was looking off in the distance. After a moment, she continued.

"He set me up in the art gallery after I got my degree. I have the soul of an artist, but the mind of a businesswoman, so I figured that running a gallery would be best for me. And while we're doing true confessions, I also need to tell you this: I am very well to do. In fact I'm rich. Weird, I've never said that; I was raised to consider talking about money as vulgar and distasteful, but I want you to know everything about me. I inherited a trust fund last year that's worth somewhere around ten million dollars. I mean, I don't live like I'm that rich, you've seen my apartment, it's nice, but it's not ten million nice." Sam looked down at his well-worn jeans and tattered sneakers. Suddenly, he felt like poor relations.

"Well, I had an idea you came from money. But I figured you ran the gallery for some rich backers. Ten million—WOW!"

"Yeah, that's why I never told you early on." Cat turned and looked directly into Sam's eyes. "It's been my experience that when people know you've got money, before they get to know you, they treat you differently. I didn't want that for *us*. The night I walked into the club at the hotel, and saw you playing the guitar and singing, I couldn't tell where the song ended, and you began. I felt like I knew you, like I had always known you." She searched his face for a glimmer of understanding.

Sam wanted to reassure her, but decided to speak candidly instead. "That's part of why I'm so confused and agitated right now. I'm confronted with some huge decisions. My daddy just killed himself and, as if that wasn't enough of a crisis, he's left me this farm, my brothers, and Grandma to take care of. All my life, he impressed upon me our connection with this land. He said it was Papa's legacy and that it was our sacred responsibility to carry on this tradition that Papa started. The funny thing is, I don't think Daddy ever really loved this place. And, from what Thad told me yesterday, Daddy wanted to escape it just as much as me and Mama. Papa fought and sweated, and kept this place solely from his hard work and ingenuity, all Daddy and I ever wanted to do was run away from it."

Sam paused and Cat searched for the right words. "I think you have a much deeper connection to this place than you know, and I know you love your brothers. Your grandma is not someone you need worry about. My impression of her is a strong, capable, and independent woman who never needed taking care of."

Sam grinned, "Yeah, she reminds me of you."

Cat stood up and brushed the hair from her face. "Well, I have always prided myself on being a self-contained unit." Her compassion was evident. "But that's all changed now. I love you

Samuel. I want what's best for you, and now, us. You make whatever decision you need to make and I will stick by you, regardless, as long as you follow your heart. You know a fellow could do a lot worse than inherit a farm and home with two loving brothers, a steamroller of a grandma, and a beautiful rich woman that loves him."

Sam beamed, stood up, and slipped his arms around her waist. "You mean if I decide to stay and run the farm, you'd stay here with me?"

"I think we could talk about it. We could work out the details, yes." Cat leaned back and gazed at Sam with new understanding. "When you got out of that cab at Penn Station and I looked into your eyes, I found something. I found something that I wasn't even looking for. I made up my mind right then that I wanted to be with you and only you, which brings us to something else we need to discuss."

"Yeah, what's that?"

"I know that we've never had a spoken commitment between us. I also know that you've seen other people while you were seeing me and I've done the same. But I stopped seeing everybody except one guy a couple weeks into you and me seeing each other. I guess I kept seeing him because I've known him awhile and he's comfortable and safe. To tell you the truth, I felt like, as long as I could continue dating him, I could keep telling myself that I wasn't falling in love with you." Sam tried to kiss her, but Cat hurried on. "Then, right after you left, I went to see him one last time and I told him that that was it. I told him I was in love..." Sam looked puzzled. "Yeah, I slept with him. I don't really know why. I guess I felt like I owed him that much." Cat's tone became matter-of-fact. "All he ever really wanted from me was my body anyway, and all I ever got from him was intelligent and interesting company. I guess you could call it an even exchange of goods and services."

Sam pulled her close, into an embrace that bordered on desperation. "I'm glad you ended it, and thank you for being honest with me. I knew all along you weren't sitting at home waiting for me to call. I knew you had someone else. And you're right, I saw other people in New York, I guess mainly because I thought, there is no way this beautiful intelligent New York City gal could ever love me. I figured I may as well play the part of the lounge musician lothario to keep my mind off the fact that you could be fucking someone else, too. But you know what? It didn't work. If I took some drunk model or cocktail waitress or stewardess or aspiring actress to bed, as soon as they left, all I could do was think about you. Where you were? Were you alone? Were you making love to someone else? Were you thinking about me? And on and on until it made me crazy!" Pleased with Sam's confession Cat smiled. "But there is one more serious thing I need to tell you and I hope you understand."

"What Sam?"

"Since I've been here, someone from my past has been coming around. You remember I told you on the phone about the psycho old girlfriend of mine?"

"Yeah, and?"

"Well, she came by the first night after I arrived. We had a couple of drinks and smoked a joint and I don't wanna' say *it* just happened, because *it* never just happens. I mean it's not like I fell down and landed in her pussy or anything, but we had sex. I knew it was a bad idea and I felt awful afterwards. But, since then, she's still coming around and acting crazy. I told her I was in love with you and to leave me alone, but she's not the type to just let things go. Anyway, I wanted to tell you because there's a good chance she'll be at the funeral and or the wake. And knowing her, she may confront you and I don't want you to be surprised." For a moment, Cat seemed deep in thought and then her face morphed into acceptance. "Cat, I'm sorry. I love you and I don't want anyone but you."

"Don't apologize, there's nothing to be sorry about. We've both been honest with each other and that's what's important." Cat stuck her hands in Sam's front pockets and looked into his eyes. "But I do want a promise from you, and I'll make the same one to you." Sam nodded. "I promise I'll never share myself with anyone but you, for as long as you want me."

Sam feigned contemplation. "Well, Miss Cat, that's gonna' be a long time. I promise you no one will ever come between us again, not now, not ever. I love you."

"And I love you, Samuel Lee Thomas."

"Are you sure you wanna' be with a Southampton County dirt farmer. If I stay here, that's all I'll ever be."

"You're way more than that Sam, and you always will be to me."

They both turned and walked back down the grassy lane towards the house to see what Zeke was doing to the battered blue pickup. Sam could hear the engine sputtering and backfiring. They approached the tractor shed and Sam yelled, "Damn! That thing's runnin' rough Zeke."

"I know Sam, but," Zeke said and grinned. "I can fix it."

"Zeke, I want you to meet my girlfriend, Cat."

Zeke's eyes got big as he stretched out his arms in Cat's direction.

Sam saw Zeke's obvious approval and said, "I know, I know, she's purty and she looks like Mama and you want a big hug." Sam laughed, "Go ahead."

"It's nice to meet you, Zeke!" Cat said. The final three words were squeaks as Zeke squeezed the air from her lungs like an old bellows.

Zeke was smiling ear to ear, as he put Cat down. He lifted the hood of the truck and, without hesitation, went to work. Zeke seemed more to Sam like a surgeon over a patient than a simple-minded mechanic.

They watched Zeke for a few minutes, and Sam said, "We gotta' go find Thad Zeke, see ya' at lunch."

"Bye Zeke." Cat waved, and they walked on.

"See what I mean? Everything on this place is falling apart. He works on that truck at least once a week. He and Lem both should be somewhere with people who are, you know, like them, learning a trade and having fun."

"What are you talking about? They both have trades and

they're damned good at em'. And they *are* with people like them; they're at home, with family, where they belong. Do you even notice the way they look at you? They see you as their big brother, their mother, and their father. I guess you've always had to be."

Sam began to walk faster. Cat hurried to keep up; she was determined to have him hear her out.

"Sam, are you listening to me? You've got to stay. You can't walk away from this. Your mom left, your daddy took his own life, none of that was your fault. It was all out of your control but this isn't! You'll forgive your mom and dad one day for what they've done, but you'll never be able to forgive yourself if you walk away from this."

Sam stopped suddenly and faced her, his face grim. "And what about my music Cat? What do I do about that? We've just been offered a recording contract. Do you have any idea how long I've dreamed about that?"

"I know that's been your dream Sam, and I'm sorry about that. But in the last few months, I've gotten to know you. I do know you, and I just want you to make this decision carefully. I'll help, but please think hard on this."

"Okay." Sam wanted her to drop it. Clasping her hand, he said, "Let's go, there's one more person I want you to meet."

They walked in silence back down the grassy strip between the fields.

As they headed towards the back woods, Sam explained, "We gotta' take the trail to Thad's house."

They came out on the other side of the woods into a small field. A little whitewashed house sat on the other side of the field facing the road. The original part of the house was old, very old. Sam guessed the early 1800s. It was probably a slave or sharecropper shack originally, but people had added parts, possibly more than once. It was now six rooms, freshly painted and neat. He and Cat walked past a small vegetable garden and a couple apple trees into the green orderly backyard. Sam heard Thad's harp and followed the sound around the house to the front porch. Thad sat with his eyes shut tight, playing his harmonica for no one but the elements. Sam and Cat sat down beside him while he finished the tune.

Cat stood up. "That was incredible!" She thrust out her hand. "Thad, I'm Cat, Sam's girlfriend. I've heard so much about you."

Thad engulfed her long delicate fingers and hand in his. "Well how do, I'm Thaddeus, farmer and harp player."

Not letting go of her palm Thad turned to Sam. "She's just as beautiful as you said, Sam. You definitely got your daddy and Papa's taste in women. She reminds me of your mama."

"Damn… you and everybody else I've introduced her to."

When Thad finally released Cat's hand, she sat back down. Then Thad began to speak to them in that mellifluous baritone of his. "There's nothing wrong with dat, your mama was a beautiful and talented woman and I expect we ain't heard da last of her yet. Hey, dat reminds me. You 'member when you wuz little and we used to play together? Your mama on da piano, you on da guitar and me on da harp? Man those was wuz some good times." Thad turned to Cat, "We used to get him ta sing and he had a big, loud, full voice. Even back den." Cat smiled at Sam.

"Yeah, I remember Thad. Sometimes… I wish I could forget."

"Why would you wanna go and do dat boy? Those are good memories. Home, family, music, seems to me that's all a man really needs. And oh yeah, a beautiful woman like Miss Cat here to share it all with. You're a lucky young man. I think it's time you start reco'nizing it."

"I remember Mama showing me a few notes on the piano, and then a few chords on the guitar and the both of ya'll always tellin' me to stand up straight and sing loud…" The final two words, "and proud!" Sam and Thad shouted in unison and laughed.

"Das all we ever had to do. You wuz born with a natchel talent, better than your mama's and better than mine. A natchel born bluesman, das what you are."

The praise made Sam uncomfortable. "Shit Thad, you're one of the most talented musicians I ever known. How come you never went out into the world and played in a blues band? You could'a been famous."

Thad looked across the road and reflected. "I did once when I was young. I went on da road wit' some fellas for six weeks. Played a bunch a juke joints down South. They used ta call it da chitlin circuit." Thad turned back to face Sam. "We even played a couple nice clubs up North, but it twon't for me." He brought the harmonica to his chest. "I never much felt da need for other folks ta love my music. I always felt like I loved it enough myself. Besides, I wuz homesick. Ya'll's my family, always have been." He smacked his hand down on the porch. "Dis is home ta me."

Just then, the screen door slammed behind them. A little boy shuffled across the porch and stood behind Thaddeus. "Grandpa?"

"Hey little man," Thad said as he swung the toddler into his lap. "Dis here is my daughter's boy, Thomas."

"Well hello Thomas." Cat smiled as she reached toward the boy. "What beautiful green eyes you have."

Sam agreed, "Yeah Thad. He's got your green eyes."

"Not just *him*. We all got 'em. Me, my daughter, my mama. It kinda makes ya wonder don't it?"

Sam lit a smoke. "I didn't know your daughter was here."

"Yeah she's been here a few months. She's in town right now gittin a few groceries."

Cat pulled the boy in her lap. "How old is Thomas Thad?" It seemed to Sam that she didn't want to ever let him go.

"He's almost two now. My daughter came down from D.C. a few months ago after her trifling boyfriend; Tom's daddy got locked up. But das okay, Grandpa's taking care of 'em now, right Tom?"

"Love you Grandpa," the little boy said.

"Aww..." Cat was in love.

"Alright baby," said Sam. "Let go of him so he can play. Your biological clock's ticking so loud it's scaring me."

They laughed.

After dinner Cat helped Grandma clean up and Sam went up to his room. The funeral was tomorrow. What was he going to do? Should he go back to New York and sign the record deal and record the album? What would happen to Grandma and Thad? They were getting old, his brothers weren't getting any younger either and for that matter neither was he. What was happening? They needed him. They all needed him, and Cat, sitting there with that green-eyed baby—there was a look on her face—something clicked in his head. He felt like they belonged here. They all belonged here.

Suddenly he went to the closet and pulled out an old guitar case. He opened it carefully. It was his first electric guitar. His dad had given it to him the Christmas after his mom left. It was an old Silvertone dad had ordered out of the Sears & Roebuck catalog. Daddy had said, "I know you really wanted one, if you take to it I'll get you a better one another Christmas." There were *some* good memories. He lifted the lid of the small compartment that held picks and strings and pulled out an envelope. He'd only read it once in his entire life. No, he wouldn't read it tonight. He placed it on the dresser and then removed one more item from the guitar case and left the room. He ran downstairs into the kitchen and kissed Grandma and Cat both on their cheeks while they stood there washing dishes and chatting.

"I'm going outside, meet me behind the barn when you're done, bye ya'll." Sam dashed out the door.

"That boy ain't right," Grandma said.

Sam walked towards the barn, he needed a smoke out of range of Grandma and he also wanted to dig out another jar of moonshine. Thad had revealed the location of the secret stash.

Cat went upstairs to freshen up before going out back to meet Sam. She brushed her teeth and hair and dabbed perfume on her neck and wrists, checked herself in the mirror and headed down the hall. She stopped at Sam's room, thought a minute and went in. She had resisted the temptation to snoop since she'd arrived, but now she couldn't help herself. She noticed the old guitar in the case, on the bed. It was open as well as the door to the small compartment. She glanced around the room: various rock stars stared at her from their posters, concert ticket stubs tacked to the bands Sam had seen, spelling bee ribbons, an old photo of a smiling elderly man in a rocking chair, he had a huge handlebar mustache and longish white hair, his eyes were big and expressive and a little intimidating, another snap-shot caught her eye, Sam and a beautiful long legged blond at the beach, they both had shiny hair, perfect teeth and brown athletic bodies. A Coppertone Ad. Then she saw it, an envelope on the dresser. It was labeled: Sam, Lem and Zeke. She knew she shouldn't, but she opened it and began to read.

Dearest Sam, Lem & Zeke,

This is harder than even I expected it would be. Mama has to leave. I cannot explain this to you all in terms that you will understand. You may never understand it. I'm not sure I understand it. That is the horrible chance I am taking in doing this. You all may never want to see me again. I may never again gaze into your eyes. I may never again rub your heads as you fall asleep. I don't know where my life will take me. That is why you guys cannot go with me. I fell in love with your father when I was very young, marriage and you boys followed quickly. I don't regret a thing. I love the three of you with all my heart, but I can't take you away from the farm. It's been your home since you were born. It's a great place to grow up.

I love your father, a part of me always will. But I can't live with him anymore. Sam, you will understand this someday and I hope you will forgive me. Your daddy will do his best and take care of you three. Don't blame him, he's a good man; just know that he loves you even when he doesn't act like it.

Sam you've got to be strong. Your brothers look up to you and they're going to need you. Have patience with your daddy, he means well.

I will keep in touch with you all and visit sometime. Be

good boys and listen to your daddy and Grandma.

I Love the Three of You to

    the Moon and Stars and Back Again,

              Mama

Summer sat alone in her room. It wasn't just a room; it was a suite of rooms over the four-car garage behind her house. She'd been living in the mother-in-law suite since she was a junior in high school. That's when it got bad. That's when she couldn't bear to live in the house with *her* anymore. That's when her mother went crazy. It happened over time, in small almost unnoticed and unrelated incidents. She'd forget to pick up Summer after Softball practice, she'd sit in the dark and talk to herself, and she'd lose her temper with the servants over some small inconsequential thing. Then came *the* night.

Summer found her in a corner of the attic wailing and disoriented. Her mother was alternately sobbing hysterically and screaming, "Get away!" The things she had said: "Get away from me you little bitch! All of you... you... little girls with your little shoes and your little gloves and your little panties and the stupid little bows in your hair," she spit and drooled as she continued her diatribe, "I was young and beautiful once! Your daddy loved me... only meeeeeeeeeeeeeeeeeeee!" She screamed and it sounded like the pain had been festering and growing inside of her for a thousand years.

Then Mama went away for a while. Not for too long. She was back in less than thirty days. Summer's daddy had said she had paranoid schizophrenia. Summer wondered why Mama walked so funny, like she couldn't quite pick her feet up. Daddy called it the Thorazine Shuffle. Mama didn't say much at all. The doctors had her on all kinds of medication: Thorazine for daytime craziness and Seconal for occasional sleeplessness caused by nighttime craziness. Summer looked at her mother sometimes and…well…she just wasn't there anymore. Her mother had checked out a long time ago and hadn't bothered to leave a forwarding address.

Summer snorted two huge lines of coke. "Shit," she hissed, stood up and started pacing. "He can't do this to me. I say when it's over, and it's not over, not by a long shot." Her life was falling apart. She had flunked out of Longwood. Daddy was threatening her with a job at his office and of all things community college. *Is he out of his mind too?*

"Summer?" Daddy was in the garage at the foot of the stairs.

"Yes Daddy?"

"Will you be having dinner with us tonight? Or are you going to see Sam?"

Great—dinner with the Judge and the drooling idiot. Since her sisters had left meals were usually with Mama and Summer alone. Mama mostly just sat, staring into space, nibbling here and there. If the Judge ate with them it was a non-stop dissertation on the never ending cavalcade of achievements accomplished by his other daughters: Meg married well, very well, a plastic surgeon out in California no less, Caroline was following in Daddy's footsteps, graduated top of her class UVA Law School and to push that dagger of overachievement in a little deeper, she went to work for the Public Defender's office in Norfolk and became a champion of the downtrodden, wasn't Daddy proud! And last, but certainly not least, there was that dike bitch sister of hers Virginia; you'd have thought equine blood flowed in her veins. She always picked the right horses to buy, to breed, to show, she was a local horseflesh celebrity. Never mind that Daddy financed every penny. He loved his horses almost as much as he did his daughters, well to hear him tell it he did, but Summer thought otherwise.

"No Daddy, no dinner and no Sam."

"I thought considering they're gonna' bury his daddy tomorrow you might want to spend some time with him tonight."

"No Daddy, Sam's got other plans."

"Well, I guess I'll see you tomorrow. Goodnight sweetheart."

"Night, Daddy." She checked herself in the mirror, a little black dress on her body and a little white powder up her nose. She downed half a glass of vodka, neat, one last glance in the mirror, *whoops*, wiped her nose, picked up her keys and headed out the door.

"Summer needs a new man," she mumbled to herself as she walked down the stairs.

Cat walked around the barn and looked for Sam, where was he? She peeked in the open door. She saw the flicker of candlelight dancing on the walls of one of the empty stalls.

There he was, standing in the middle of the stall, the soft light bathed him in an unreal glow, Cat felt a little dizzy, he dropped to one knee and held up a little black box, "What are you doing?" she asked. She felt faint.

"Cat, I love you, the moment I saw you at the airport I knew I could never be without you." He opened the box. "Mama gave this to me, a few weeks before she left. I've kept it all these years. Daddy never even knew I had it. Mama told me to give this to the girl I wanted to marry. She said just make sure you want her to have it forever. Cat, will you marry me?"

She couldn't think. She couldn't breathe. Was he crazy? She didn't hesitate, she said it, "Yes, yes Samuel I'll marry you, but are you sure, are you sure this is what you want?"

"I've never been surer of anything in my life. I want to stay here and help my brothers and live with you and make babies and farm and play music with Thad. This is home. This is where I belong, but it won't be right without you, are you sure you can handle life down here, being a Manhattan girl and all."

"I'll have to go to New York once or twice a month for a couple days and twice a year for a week or more, but I love it down here and like I've already told you I want to cruise the back roads for some new folk artist talent, so I'll have plenty to do around here. This feels like home to me too Sam, it has since I got here. I love your brothers, I love your grandma, I love Thad and his grandson, and I love the house, the land and the animals. There's no where I'd rather be."

"Then it's a deal."

"It's a deal."

They kissed, and hugged, and stripped each other very slowly.

Summer stirred from sleep, it was 4:54 a.m. and she wouldn't have been a bit surprised if her head had split open and released a vodka and cocaine induced demon. She rolled over and looked at him: nice body, nice face, well equipped below the waist, nice apartment, nice car, good coke, good job, good family, good God! She sounded like her mother. This wasn't what she wanted. He, it, this thing beside her wasn't what she wanted. She wanted Sam. She had to get home and get some sleep. She had to be cute and quick witted tomorrow, today, in a few hours. She would have a talk with little Miss Yankee Bitch. She'd tell her things that would make her run back to New York like she stole something. *Sam loves me.* Summer would convince his little girlfriend of it, and when she was gone… Sam would be pissed, but Summer could bring him around. It wouldn't take long; she knew what to do.

She found everything but her panties, got dressed and slipped out.

It was a beautiful April morning. Sam's head was still a little foggy from the moonshine. He sat up, "Damn," he moaned. He was also a little sore, a sweet ache between his legs, deep in his pubic bone. He smiled. He and Cat must have gotten athletic last night, too bad he didn't remember much of it. It was 9:10 A.M. Why hadn't Grandma woke him? His door opened and Cat slid in.

"Morning babe," she said and kissed him on the forehead.

"Good morning my fiancée. I wasn't dreaming was I, you did agree to be my wife last night?"

"Yes Sam, I did."

"Cool, why didn't Grandma wake us for breakfast?"

"She said she figured we could use the rest. She's keeping breakfast warm in the oven. Your brothers are doing the morning chores."

"I'm starved, let's go eat."

"Okay, but first I need to tell you something. I read the letter from your mom. I read it last night. I hope you're not angry. I couldn't help it. I want to know everything about you and she's part of you."

"It's okay. I almost read it last night myself. I've only read it once, when I was nine."

"Oh Sam, you've got to read it again. She loved you... I mean she loves you guys. I don't know why she didn't keep in touch but there has to be a good reason."

Sam took Cat's hand and said, "Come on, I want to show you something." He led her up a narrow switchback staircase into the attic. There were four rooms off the main hall and they went into a small one in the back corner.

"My God," Cat gasped and stood there with her mouth open.

There were paintings everywhere: hanging, leaning against walls, and one on an easel half done. They were big brilliant landscapes and portraits done in a primitive childlike style. They told stories, stories of simple country people, their dignity, their misfortune, their hopes, their failures—and their broken hearts.

"Who Sam, who did these?" The style seemed vaguely familiar but she was overcome with emotion and on the verge of tears.

"My mom. My mama painted these. She stopped about a year before she left and she never came up here again. It's funny, when I got older, I'd sneak up here sometimes and just stare at 'em. Like I thought if I stared at 'em long enough, I'd get it. I'd understand why she left. The older I got, I think I did sort of understand. I understood that if she left so she could do this again... if she were somewhere painting and smiling like she did when I was a kid, then it was okay, it still hurt like hell, but it was okay."

"What's your mom's name?"

"Josephine, Josephine Thomas."

"What was her maiden name?"

"Stewart, Josie Stewart."

"I knew it, I know *your* mom. I've sold several of her paintings. I've been to her house in the Catskills. Your *mother* is Josephine Stewart!"

The plane took off from Albany at 9:25 a.m. She was going home. She held the newspaper with his obituary in it. She had the *Southampton News* mailed to her in the Catskills. Why had they never replied to any of her letters? Why had they never returned her calls? After a few years she had given up. It hurt too much to make the effort anymore. Henry was dead. Had he been lying and deliberately keeping the boys from her? Worse yet, had he poisoned them against her? Did her boys hate her? She had to find out; once and for all she had to know. She had a family. She missed them. She loved them and she was going to get them back or know the reason why.

Thaddeus shined his shoes while his grandson played on the front porch. His daughter was at her job in Franklin. He couldn't stop thinking about what was said yesterday about their green eyes. He'd never thought much of it. His mama never did tell him who his daddy was, but that never much mattered to Thaddeus. Papa always treated him like a son, taught him to farm, fish and hunt. Sam's dad Henry always treated him like a brother, gave him this house when he and Josie moved to the big house after Papa died. He looked at the baby, those eyes, then it struck him... they looked like Papa's, not so much the color, Papa's were more gray, no... more like wet steel, but in fix and intensity the little boy had Papa's eyes. Thaddeus went into the house and looked in the mirror; Papa's mesmerizing stare looked back at him.

Grandma and Cat were getting the boys dressed. "Now you boys know what you gotta' do, you gotta' tote your daddy's casket from the altar to the hearse and then from the hearse to the grave. You're pallbearers, that's a big 'sponsibility. Just do what Sam does and you'll be fine."

"They'll do fine Grandma. These are two handsome, intelligent gentlemen aren't you guys?" Cat smiled and Lem and Zeke both blushed. They weren't used to compliments, especially not from a stunning young woman. Cat finished straightening their ties. "There… perfect." Cat kissed them both on the cheek.

Lem grabbed her hand and said, "Miss Cat, Zeke and me wuz talkin' and we… uhhh… well… we want you and Sam to stay here with us. Mama left a long time ago and Sam left after that and now Daddy's gone and we want you and Sam to stay."

He started crying and Cat hugged him and said, "It's okay Lem, it's okay, we're staying. Sam and I are staying."

"Thank the Lord," Grandma cried as she smiled through the tears. "I knew Sam would do the right thing." They all four hugged and cried. Grandma looked at Cat's left hand on Zeke's shoulder and she knew, she had given that ring back to Papa to give to Sam's dad for Josie when they got married. Three generations of Thomas women had worn that ring and now it was on the ring finger of Sam's fiancée.

"Everything's gonna' be just fine, this family's gonna' be happy again, I know it, I just know it."

It was 12:22 P.M.; Josephine Stewart got in her rental car and left Norfolk Airport. She had an hour and forty minutes to prepare her to face almost fifteen years of questions and guilt. Would they be glad to see her or would they turn her away? It didn't matter, she had to know and she had to say goodbye to Henry. *Poor Henry, all he ever wanted was to join the military and see the world.* Instead he'd been blindsided: by the business of running a farm, marriage, children and by a legacy, a legacy he never wanted and couldn't live up to.

Summer stepped out of the shower, slick and wet. She looked in the mirror: five hours of sleep, was that enough? She was going to have to do the makeup job of her life to cover those dark circles. Everything was going to be fine, she'd get rid of her competition and Sam would be hers. He had always loved her. They'd stay here until she was twenty-five and then Daddy would give her her trust fund and they'd travel. They'd just take off— go everywhere and do everything. She couldn't wait to shake the dirt of this backwards ass county off of her feet for good.

She snorted two small lines and began applying her

makeup. She'd wear her other little black dress today, the one that was slightly longer, mid-calf, split up the back just high enough, mid-thigh, and tight enough to give the impression of over ripened fruit that was ready to burst. She had dangerous but dignified curves in that dress and she intended to use every one of them today.

Sam and Thad stood in front of the church talking. "Thad, I gotta' tell you a couple things. First, I'm staying; I can't leave the boys, Grandma and you. This is where I want to be. And second, I asked Cat to marry me last night and she said yes. She's gonna' be my wife and stay here with us."

"Lawd have mercy! Maybe this won't be such a sad day after all." He hugged Sam, gave him one of Lem and Zeke's big bear hugs, "Boy, I knew you'd do the right thang, ooooweeee, and you sho' nuf picked a good one. Miss Cat is one helluva woman, 'scuse me Lord. What'd you do about the other one, you took care of it didn't you?"

"Who knows with Summer Thad? But I'm covered, I told Cat the truth, just in case Summer shows up today and starts trouble; there's nothing she can tell Cat that she don't already know."

"Good boy, your daddy and I taught you well."

"You Thad, not Daddy, there were a whole lot of things we counted on gettin' from you that Daddy couldn't or wouldn't give us. You know I've never thanked you for all the kind words and deeds that you gave us over the years. The half of Daddy that was missing you way more than made up for, thank you."

"Oh hush boy, I didn't do nuttin for ya'll I wouldn't do for my own. Your Papa and your daddy always treated me like family and truth is I always thought of you and your brothers as my boys, and besides young boys caint have too many folks that love 'em, and believe me you boys weren't always easy to love."

"Why'd he do it Thad? Why? Why now? Why like this?"

"I caint answer all dem questions Mistah Sam, yo' daddy was a good man and he did the best he could. You know some folk's say the good Lord don't put no more on ya than ya can bear, but I ain't sure tis so. Papa left him some big shoes to fill and your mama left a mighty big hole in his heart and I think it was more than he could bear. But he's okay now. He's standing on the bow of some tall ship, flying across the ocean like a gull. He's finally gonna' get to see those exotic ports o' call. Now there's something I gotta' tell you. Your grandma evidently called Mr. Silas, the undertaker, and told him if he could make your daddy presentable, to leave the casket open for thirty minutes prior to the service."

"She did what? She and Silas too, for that matter, both knew I wanted it closed, how good could Silas possibly make him look? Daddy blew his face off with a shotgun!"

"Now calm down Mistah Sam it don't do no good goin' and getting' all riled up. You know how your grandma is, she's done gone and got it in her head that folks should be able to say good-bye face to face if they want to."

"So help me Thad if I hear one person say he looks good… if I hear one person say he looks peaceful I'm gonna' fucking flip! If Silas has got him all made up like a dime store whore with pink lipstick and bulletproof pancake makeup I'm gonna' choke what little if any life there is left in the man, out of him! I may have had issues with my dad, but I did mean to spare him this last indignity." Sam stomped off towards the door of the church and Thad stopped him.

"Now don't go making a fuss at the church Sam. That temper of yours is gonna' get you in trouble one day. Go in there and look for yourself. He looks g… I mean he looks like your daddy, but if you don't think so tell Silas to close the casket nicely and I'm sure he will. Remember, you're in charge now, and you can get things done your way without beating people over the head with your temper."

Sam took a deep breath, calmed down a notch, and went in the church. He immediately heard a commotion in front of the altar.

"That's Papa's ring, he promised it to me. Henry claimed it had been misplaced, the rapscallion, he thought everything was his just because he stayed on the farm. I got nothing when Papa died, nothing!"

Sam knew who it was instantly: his whiny Aunt Gladys and her older sister Fannie, his dad's sisters. "What's goin' on Aunt Gladys? Why are you crying and taking on?"

Now Gladys was bent over the casket trying to pull the ring off his daddy's pinkie finger. "Now hold on a minute Gladys. Daddy always wore that ring when he got dressed up and Grandma figured he'd want to be buried with it on, but if you want it that bad we'll have it removed before they close the casket and give it to you."

"No we will not Samuel Lee Thomas! You touch that ring Gladys and I'll snatch you bald-headed and believe me it won't take but a minute!"

Oh shit, it's Grandma. Where'd she come from?

"Calm down Grandma, I'll take care of this. Where's Silas?"

"Right behind you sir."

Damn, how did he do that? Snuck up on me like a ghost.

"Silas step over here and let's discuss this."

They walked over to the side entrance and Sam watched as Silas glided like a ghoul: a cemetery specter.

"Have it removed when you close the casket and give it to me quietly."

"Yes Mr. Thomas," Silas lisped.

"Thank you."

Sam walked back to the casket. "See me at the wake Aunt Gladys. I'll give you the ring." It was only a ring, and somehow *things* didn't seem important anymore.

"Grandma, where are Cat and the boys?"

"In the parlor, Cat's still fussing over Zeke's hair."

His work here was done anyway. He was in charge now and he was going to start acting like it. Thaddeus always gave good advice, all Sam had to do was ask and things would be done his way. Sam was beginning to like this. "I'm going to check on them Grandma, hold down the fort."

"Don't worry Son; I've been getting the better of these two

for over thirty years."

Fannie released an audible, "Humph."

The boys were sitting in the parlor looking particularly uncomfortable. Cat greeted Sam at the door and kissed him on the cheek, "Everything okay?"

"No, but I'm learning to deal with it anyway."

"Good."

Josephine stepped out of the non-descript four-door sedan and into the street. This would be the first time she'd seen her boys in almost fifteen years, the first and possibly the last. She walked up the sidewalk to the side parlor door entrance. She reached for the knob…

"I'm gonna' step outside and grab a smoke," Sam reached for the door. Before he could get his hand on the knob it opened.

"Mama?"

"Sam?"

"Mama!" Lem and Zeke yelled simultaneously and stampeded towards their mother.

"Josephine?" Cat's mouth hung open.

"Cat?" Josephine looked genuinely puzzled now.

Sam got out of the way and his brothers proceeded to squeeze the life out of their mother. All three cried, a continuous stream, their cheeks shiny with tears.

Cat hugged Sam and wept quietly.

Sam broke the silence, "Geez you guys, let her go."

Josephine looked at Sam, "Son," she stretched out her arms…

"We get ready to bury one and the other one comes *back* to life." There were so many things he wanted to say, so many questions to ask, but not right now. His mama was here, and they had to go and bury Daddy.

"Mama." Then Sam went to her, into her arms and one tear from each eye rolled down his cheeks. He was determined to hold himself together today regardless the situation or this surprise.

"Its okay baby, I know you've got a lot of questions and I'll try to answer them all, but right now let's go bury your daddy."

Damn, she's definitely my mother.

Sam released Josephine and finished composing himself. He looked in his mother's eyes and said, "My room, before the wake, we'll talk, let's go."

They all walked down the hall to the sanctuary. They entered and sat in the family pew. Grandma was already seated when Josephine sat down right beside her, "Oh my word!" Grandma gasped, "Lord have mercy as I live and breathe its Josephine, Josephine Thomas, I mean Stewart. Lord this day is gonna' give me the palpitations yet! Between Henry's greedy sisters and now *you*…Josephine I just don't know what to say."

"Good Grandma, 'cause none of us are gonna' say anything till later okay?" Sam whispered. "Where's Thaddeus?"

"Somewhere in the back."

"I'm going to get him, he's gonna' sit with us. He's family too and he's the only one, including me, who has yet to run out on us despite our madness." Sam walked to the back and fetched Thaddeus.

As they walked up the aisle, Thad asked, "Was that your mama I just saw walking in with ya'll?"

"Yes Thad it was, it seems this day is just chock full of surprises."

"Ain't it though? You know folks is gonna' talk even more with me sittin' up front with ya'll."

"Let 'em talk Thad, you're as much family as any of 'em and more than most."

Thad sat down beside Josephine, "Good to see you Miss Josie."

"Thad, good to see you too," she kissed him on the cheek.

"Lawd you done gone and kissed a black man in da Baptist Church."

"I don't care; if they want to talk I want to make sure we give them plenty to talk about."

"Oh they gots plenty to talk about now Miss Josie, they sho' nuf do. I had a feeling we might be seeing you today."

"It was long overdue Thad, long overdue."

The preacher made his way over to the pulpit and the rustling and murmurs from the crowd subsided.

"We are gathered here today to send one of God's servants home…" the preacher droned.

Sam's mind wandered. Daddy hadn't stepped foot in this church since Mama left, and he didn't hardly go then except for holidays and funerals. No, he never had much use for the church or church folks. Daddy used to say, "When a common thief robs you, he tells you he's robbing you. A preacher or deacon will smile in your face, shake your hand, tell you the Lord loves you and 'spect you to be happy about the fact that he's got his other hand in your back pocket stealing your wallet." Sam smiled.

Half of the people here never had a kind word for his daddy when he was alive. They only showed up now so they could pat themselves on the back later and say they paid their respects to the dead.

Funerals are definitely for the living.

He had heard people say it, but he had never fully understood it until now. The worse was yet to come. They'd line up after the graveside service and do that awkward shake of your hand and that gratuitous, "I'm so sorry," as if they had some personal responsibility for his daddy's death.

The preacher's monotonous drone continued, empty words meant to console and placate. Reverend Williams didn't even know Daddy; most of the people here never said anything to Sam's dad in public and what they said about him in private was less than kind.

No one noticed the tall, leggy blond in the black dress and dark glasses slip in the front door and sit in the back pew. Summer crossed her legs and sighed, "I hate these fuckin' things," she whispered to herself. She only had to endure the rest of the funeral and short graveside service and then she'd have her say at the wake. She stared at the back of Cat's head. *Nice hair, dark—I bet she's hairy as shit. How can Sam fuck her after having me?*

A hymn, a prayer, and that was it, the funeral was over.

Sam, his brothers and Thad walked up to the casket and

began their pall bearing duties.

Well Daddy, this is the first half of our last walk together.

They carried the box their father was in down the aisle, as they got to the door Sam noticed Summer in the last pew. She took off her sunglasses, looked into his eyes and smiled—predator and prey.

The ride to the cemetery was mercifully brief. Cat and Josephine monopolized the conversation; catching up on why this coincidence, the two of them seeing each other here, had taken place.

The second half of Sam's last walk with his dad began…Sam was five…

"Hey Daddy?"

"Yeah Son?"

"You gonna' show me how to clean the fish we caught?"

"Yeah Sam."

"And then Mama's gonna' cook 'em?"

"Yeah Mama's gonna' cook 'em."

"And then me and Lem and Zeke are gonna' eat 'em all up."

"Can you and your brother's share with me and your mama and Thad and Grandma?"

"Yeah, we can share."

Sam's dad tousled his hair and said, "Sam?"

"Yeah Dad?"

"I love you."

They sat the casket down on the lowering device. Sam rubbed the lid and whispered, "I love you too Dad, I love you too."

After the obligatory hand shaking and insincere condolence making they were off to the house for the wake. Sam had made up his mind that after the conversation he had to have with his mom they were all going to celebrate: no long faces and maudlin toasts. They were going to have a party. Sam hoped Summer didn't show up; one of her displays would definitely dampen the festivities.

Sam and his mom walked up the steps to his room. He had

thought about what he would say for years, should this day ever come, but now that she was standing in front of him he had only one question. All the angry accusations he had carried around for over a decade were reduced to one question.

"Why Mama? Not why did you leave, you could give me many reasons for that, most of which I already know. You could tell me that it was because this place and Daddy were suffocating. You could say you had to leave so you could paint again, which from what Cat has said you've been quite successful at it. I understand those things. I've felt them all myself. I know the role of the suffering artist. I've lived it. But I don't understand why you never wrote, you never called, you never came to see us once. We were little boys. We needed you! Lem and Zeke needed you! I needed you! You told me to be strong and I was, but *I needed you! I'm* okay with why you left—I understand it. But that little boy, that nine-year-old-little-boy-I-was-then, he doesn't understand. He doesn't understand all the birthdays and ballgames and holidays and graduations, all the times he looked in the stands or the hallway or down the lane out there knowing, just knowing you'd show up, you'd be here. That little boy's still here Mama! He's right here… and he needs to understand! He needs to know why!"

She was glad he had stopped talking because she couldn't bear another word. She wiped the tears from her face, smoothed her dress and said, "Sam, you're wrong. I did write. I did call. I never received a reply from any of my letters and never talked to anyone on the phone but your dad and all he would ever say was that you guys didn't want to talk to me and then he'd hang up. So eventually I stopped trying. It hurt too much. But I did send you a graduation present."

"No you didn't, I never got a letter or anything from you all this time."

"*Your daddy*, I thought all along he was keeping the mail and phone calls from you three and I wanted to pay a surprise visit, but I was scared. I was frightened to death that I'd get here and you would say horrible things to me and tell me to go away. I couldn't risk that. The memories I had of you boys were precious.

I could picture you running through the fields, fishing by the pond, playing ball, you strumming your guitar and singing. Those memories kept me going. They sustained me."

"So you think Daddy kept the letters and the calls from us?"

"He kept more than that! I sent you a guitar for your graduation and a round trip ticket to Albany to visit me, if you wanted to."

"A guitar?"

"Yeah, a '57 Stratocaster I found at an estate sale in the Catskills, it was two-tone sunburst."

"Dammit Daddy," Sam hissed.

Sam and his mom both pondered the guitar for a moment and shouted, "The study!" and they hurried downstairs.

Sam entered the kitchen a little short of breath. "Grandma where's the key to the study?"

"In the kitchen drawer I 'spose, what ya'll all in an uproar about?"

"Nothing Grandma, Mama and I'll be done in a minute."

They went down the side hall to the study. Daddy always kept it locked, because of the guns, but Sam knew; Daddy drank in there—and in the smokehouse. Neither Sam nor his brothers had been in the study since they were kids.   Unless they had done something wrong, then they were summoned and forced to stand in front of the tall desk and have Daddy look down on them and pronounce sentence. It was a ritual that Daddy inherited from Papa. The guitar, Sam had to find the guitar and prove his mother right.   He looked around the room. *Where? Where could Daddy have hidden a guitar?* Josephine stood in the doorway. *The gun cabinet.* "Where did Daddy keep the key to the gun cabinet?"

Josephine scratched her head, "Your dad, if I remember correctly was always a creature of habit, he kept everything in the same place and double checked to make sure it was there even if he had just put it there himself… so… that means the key to the gun cabinet is over the doorjamb, left end."

Sam reached over the door and plucked the key from the

jamb, "Damn, right on."

"Yeah, other than you and your brothers I expect I know your father better than most."

Sam stuck the key in the lock, turned it and opened the door. His heart sank, "Shit, just the guns." He moved back to the center of the room and scanned the entire space. *Where is it? It's got to be here.*

"Wait a minute!" Sam shouted. He looked behind the gun cabinet between the wall and the back of the cabinet, there it was. "Help me slide this cabinet out, Mom." They slid it a few inches from the wall. Sam reached behind it and pulled out a dusty hard shell guitar case. He pulled out his handkerchief and wiped down both sides of the case quickly and laid it down on the desk. He opened it slowly. It was perfect, vintage and flawless. He traced the lines of the body with his fingertips. He was overwhelmed. How much this guitar would have meant to him when it was sent. How much it meant to him now—knowing she had sent it.

This time Sam gave his mother one of Lem and Zeke's bear hugs, lifting her off the ground and spinning her around until they were both light-headed.

Thad called from the hallway, "Mr. Sam, you better get out here."

"What's wrong Thad?" Sam asked.

"Nothing yet, but Miss Summer just got here and I don't like the look she got in her eyes."

"Where is she?"

"In the kitchen with Miss Cat."

"Shit, Thad go back in there and keep an eye on both of them for me, I'll be right there."

Josephine looked puzzled, "What's wrong son? What's going on with Summer?"

"Nothing Mama, you remember how she was always…a little pushy."

"Son, that girl decided when she was just a little teeny thing that you belonged to her, at least when she wanted you to anyway. I never trusted or liked her fast little ass."

Josephine walked out of the study first and then Sam. They hurried down the hall and into the kitchen.

Grandma stood there with her hands on her hips while Thad looked like he was ready to pounce on whichever girl snapped first. Summer was saying something to Cat too quietly to decipher.

"Well, I take it everyone's been introduced," Sam said awkwardly.

"That's it!" Cat yelled and grabbed Summer by the ponytail and pulled her towards the backdoor.

"I'll take that as a yes," Sam mumbled and started across the room.

Cat shot Sam a look, "You stay right there Samuel! I'll handle this."

"Sam I think you…"

Sam interrupted his mother. "Mom, let them settle this outside. Hell, this is the country and I don't expect it's the first time this has happened on this property."

"Let me go bitch!" Summer was struggling. Cat folded Summer's arm behind her back and applied a little expert leverage. "Owww!" Summer screamed. Cat was athletic, strong and angry.

"Mr. Sam you want me to…"

"No Thad, stay put and let them have it out."

"Come on, we're going to have a little talk." Cat let go of Summer's hair and opened the door. She hustled Summer down the steps.

"Keep an eye on 'em Thad, don't let it get out of hand."

"I won't Mr. Sam," Thad said grinning.

Once in the backyard Cat pushed Summer hard, face first into the driveway.

"I could kick your ass right now in front of everybody, but I won't. Not because I'm a lady and above it, but because I've got more respect for the people I love and the memory of Sam's dad. You think you can say those nasty little things to me. You think you can give me graphic little details about Sam's lovemaking skills and that's going to make me run back to New York with my tail between my legs. I know everything and I do mean everything there is to know about Sam's sexual techniques, and do you know why? Because I taught him most of them, that's why! You see I'm a twenty-six year old woman and you're a pathetic, scared, spoiled rotten little girl throwing a temper tantrum because you can't get what you want. You're no threat to me."

Summer sat up: her knees skinned, her dress torn up to the waist and her chin and nose scraped. She crumbled. Defeated.

Before Cat went back in the house she stuck her left ring finger in Summer's face and said, "And oh yeah, by the way, I'll soon be the mistress of this house and property so run along and don't come back. You're not welcome here anymore!"

Summer collected her things: purse, sunglasses, shoes, what was left of her dignity and got in her car and fishtailed down the lane. Gone.

After humphing all the way across the driveway Aunt Gladys and Fannie came in the back door behind Cat, "Quite a display Sam, quite a display," Gladys said. Fannie just shook her head.

"Gladys, Fannie, this is my fiancée Catherine." Sam smiled.

"Well I never," Fannie snorted.

"I never thought I'd find a woman like this either Aunt Fannie," and he kissed Cat full on the mouth.

"Ooooooooweeee...I ain't never seen Miss Summer turn tail and run like that from nothing. Yeah Mr. Sam you got something there, that's a woman, a bonafide country crazy woman!" Thad laughed.

"Why thank you Thad. I love you too." Cat kissed him on the cheek.

"So how we gon' top that Mr. Sam?" Thad grinned.

"Thad, I got an idea. Do the Drake boys across the road still have drums and a bass?"

"Yeah, I thinks so."

"Well go over there and holler at 'em and tell 'em to bring their instruments and come on over. We're gonna' play some music."

"Sounds like my kinda party! Should I go fetch a couple jars o' shine?"

"Thad once again you're reading my mind but you better make it a few jars. Remember this party is in honor of my daddy! Listen up everybody!" Sam walked into the dining room. "As the new man of the house I wanna' make an announcement. From this point on today we're having a party, a celebration of Daddy's life and the lives of his children and Papa and the rest of our family, all of it," he grabbed his mom and Thad's hands. "We are also celebrating an addition to this family, my fiancée Catherine who has been a great help to me in the last few days and has agreed to be my wife and make my life complete. So everybody eat and drink and come outside in a little while and I think we're gonna' have some music for ya'll."

Grandma watched through the kitchen window as Sam, Thad and the Drake boys played music on the small rise of grass in front of the tractor shed. Grandma had never seen Sam happier or more handsome. Lem, Zeke and their mom were all singing along with Sam and Thad. Cat was holding Thad's grandson Thomas and dancing. Thad's daughter was talking to Gladys and Fannie and swaying to the music. Numerous other relatives and friends of the family were milling about singing, dancing, clapping and drinking. Grandma saw someone come into view through the bottom right corner of the window. Summer. She was holding the Judge's pistol. Grandma watched, frozen at the kitchen window like a mannequin; it took only a few seconds to unfold and Grandma saw it all in slow motion.

Summer was thirty yards from where the band was set up. She squeezed off round after round, slow and methodical. The first two shots went high and sailed harmlessly over everyone's heads. Thad ran across the bandstand towards Sam. The second two volleys spun Sam around and his shirt went crimson just as Thaddeus got there and blocked Summer's next three shots. Cat handed Josephine the baby and ran towards Sam and Thad just as they fell on top of each other—the ground around them red and wet. Zeke let out a blood-curdling scream and took off running towards Summer.

Summer released her last two rounds in Cat's direction just as Zeke got to her and knocked her to the ground.

"Get off me you fucking retard! I gotta' reload!" Summer struggled under Zeke's weight.

Sam lay on his back: he looked at the sky, it didn't hurt, nothing hurt, all he felt was wet and sleepy. He managed to whisper, "You okay Thad?" and then... He thought there was suppose to be a light—there was only dark.

THOMASTON: 1978

Two little boys played in a grassy field, one white, one black; neither noticed the difference or the similarity.

"Hey Thad, what's your grandma painting?" asked the black one.

"Your grandpa," answered the white one.

Josephine sat in the field and painted a portrait of Thaddeus, from memory. He took three bullets in the back—for Sam—that day. Lem, Zeke and Josephine rushed them to the hospital. The doctors couldn't save Thaddeus; one of the bullets punctured his heart.

"Stop bugging grandma and go help daddy chop wood," Cat told little Thad. She got a flesh wound that day, a bullet cut across her shoulder blade. She watched Sam as he cut wood, his body shiny with sweat from the hot sun. She looked at the two puckered bullet scars on his brown rib cage—the ones she kissed every night before they went to sleep. The bullets had gone in and out of his lower left lung and just missed his heart and spine. He coughed blood the entire way to the hospital. Cat held Sam and Thad's hands during the ride. About half-way there Thaddeus let go, pressed his harmonica to his chest and whispered, "Give this to little Thomas and tell Sam to teach him to play it, loud...and... proud."

Sam and Cat's son, little Thad asked his grandma, "You almost finished?"

"Yes baby, I gotta' get your Uncle Thad's eyes just right. Sam, how is Summer doing at the Sanitarium?" She pleaded insanity and was sent to Eastern State until she was deemed no risk to herself or others. Sam figured she'd be home eventually—doing the Thorazine shuffle with her mama. He supposed that was punishment enough.

"I guess she's doing as well as can be expected."

Josephine stood up and stepped away from the easel, "Okay, everybody come look—I'm done!"

They all gathered around in front of the painting and Cat gasped, "Josephine… it's perfect!"

The brilliant sun-lit landscape of the very same field they were standing in was in the background. Thaddeus stood there, Fedora cocked to one side grinning, bright white teeth and those eyes, Papa and Daddy's eyes.

"Where shall we hang it?" Josephine asked.

"Over the mantle, right between Papa and Daddy," Sam said.

Then he went back to chopping wood.

All Rights Reserved G.R.O'Berry 2005